THE DOUBLE GARDEN

NOBEL PRIZE IN LITERATURE

MAURICE MAETERLINCK

Translated by ALEXANDER TEIXEIRA DE MATTOS
Translated by ALFRED SUTRO
Illustrated by CECIL ALDIN

ALICIA EDITIONS

To my friend Cyriel Buysse.

M.M.

CONTENTS

ON THE DEATH OF A LITTLE DOG

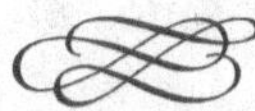

TRANSLATED BY ALEXANDER TEIXEIRA DE MATTOS, ILLUSTRATED BY CECIL ALDIN.

I

I have lost, within these last few days, a little bull-dog. He had just completed the sixth month of his brief existence. He had no history. His intelligent eyes opened to look out upon the world, to love mankind, then closed again on the cruel secrets of death.

The friend who presented me with him had given him, perhaps by antiphrasis, the startling name of Pelléas. Why rechristen him? For how can a poor dog, loving, devoted, faithful, disgrace the name of a man or an imaginary hero?

Pelléas had a great bulging, powerful forehead, like that of Socrates or Verlaine; and, under a little black nose, blunt as a churlish assent, a pair of large hanging and symmetrical chops, which made his head a sort of massive, obstinate, pensive and three-cornered menace. He was beautiful after the manner of a beautiful, natural monster that has complied strictly with the laws of its species. And what a smile of attentive obligingness, of incorruptible innocence, of affectionate submission, of boundless gratitude and total self-abandonment lit up, at the least caress, that adorable mask of ugliness! Whence exactly did that smile emanate? From the ingenuous and melting eyes? From the ears pricked up to catch the words of man? From the forehead that unwrinkled to appreciate and love, or from the stump of a tail that wriggled at the other end to testify to the intimate and impassioned joy that filled his small being, happy once more to encounter the hand or the glance of the god to whom he surrendered himself?

Pelléas was born in Paris, and I had taken him to the country. His bonny fat paws, shapeless and not yet stiffened, carried slackly through the unexplored pathways of his new existence his huge and serious head, flat-nosed and, as it were, rendered heavy with thought.

For this thankless and rather sad head, like that of an over-worked child, was beginning the overwhelming work that oppresses every brain at the start of life. He had, in less than five or six weeks, to get into his mind, taking shape within it, an image and a satisfactory conception of the universe. Man, aided by all the knowledge of his own elders and his brothers, takes thirty or forty years to outline that conception, but the humble dog has to unravel it for himself in a few days: and yet, in the eyes of a god, who should know all things, would it not have the same weight and the same value as our own?

It was a question, then, of studying the ground, which can be scratched and dug up and which sometimes reveals surprising things; of casting at the sky, which is uninteresting, for there is nothing there to eat, one glance that does away with it for good and all; of discovering the grass, the admirable and green grass, the springy and cool grass, a field for races and sports, a friendly and boundless bed, in which lies hidden the good and wholesome couch-grass. It was a question, also, of taking promiscuously a thousand urgent and curious observations. It was necessary, for instance, with no other guide than pain, to learn to calculate the height of objects from the top of which you can jump into space; to convince yourself that it is vain to pursue birds who fly away and that you are unable to clamber up trees after the cats who defy you there; to distinguish between the sunny spots where it is delicious to sleep and the patches of shade in which you shiver; to remark with stupefaction that the rain does not fall inside the houses, that water is cold, uninhabitable and dangerous, while fire is beneficent at a distance, but terrible when you come too near; to observe that the meadows, the farm-yards and sometimes the roads are haunted by giant creatures with threatening horns, creatures good-natured, perhaps, and, at any rate, silent, creatures who allow you to sniff at them a little curiously without taking offence, but who keep their real thoughts to themselves. It was necessary to learn, as the result of painful and humiliating experiment, that you are not at liberty to obey all nature's laws without distinction in the dwelling of the gods; to recognize that the kitchen is the privileged and most agreeable spot in that divine dwelling, although you are hardly allowed to abide in it because of the cook, who is a considerable, but jealous power; to learn that doors are important and capricious volitions, which sometimes lead to felicity, but which most often, hermetically closed, mute and stern, haughty and heartless, remain deaf to all entreaties; to admit, once and for all, that the essential good things of life, the indisputable blessings, generally imprisoned in pots and stewpans, are almost always inaccessible; to know how to look at them with laboriously-acquired indifference and to practise to take no notice of them, saying to yourself that here are objects which are probably sacred, since merely to skim them with the tip of a respectful tongue is enough to let loose the unanimous anger of all the gods of the house.

And then, what is one to think of the table on which so many things happen that cannot be guessed; of the derisive chairs on which one is forbidden to sleep; of the plates and dishes that are empty by the time that one can get at them; of the lamp that drives away the dark?... How many orders, dangers, prohibitions, problems, enigmas has one not to classify in one's overburdened memory!... And how to reconcile all this with other laws, other enigmas, wider and more imperious, which one bears within one's self, within one's instinct, which spring up and develop from one hour to the other, which come from the depths of time and the race, invade the blood, the muscles and the nerves and suddenly assert themselves more irresistibly and more powerfully than pain, the word of the master himself, or the fear of death?

Thus, for instance, to quote only one example, when the hour of sleep has struck for men, you have retired to your hole, surrounded by the darkness, the silence and the formidable solitude of the night. All is sleep in the master's house. You feel yourself very small and weak in the presence of the mystery. You know that the gloom is peopled with foes who hover and lie in wait. You suspect the trees, the passing wind and the moonbeams. You would like to hide, to suppress yourself by holding your breath. But still the watch must be kept; you must, at the least sound, issue from your retreat, face the invisible and bluntly disturb the imposing silence of the earth, at the risk of bringing down the whispering evil or crime upon yourself alone. Whoever the enemy be, even if he be man, that is to say, the very brother of the god whom it is your business to defend, you must attack him blindly, fly at his throat, fasten your perhaps sacrilegious teeth into human flesh, disregard the spell of a hand and voice similar to those of your master, never be silent, never attempt to escape, never allow yourself to be tempted or bribed and, lost in the night without help, prolong the heroic alarm to your last breath.

There is the great ancestral duty, the essential duty, stronger than death, which not even man's will and anger are able to check. All our humble history, linked with that of the dog in our first struggles against every breathing thing, tends to prevent his forgetting it. And when, in our safer dwelling-places of to-day, we happen to punish him for his untimely zeal, he throws us a glance of astonished reproach, as though to point out to us that we are in the wrong and that, if we lose sight of the main clause in the treaty of alliance which he made with us at the time when we lived in caves, forests and fens, he continues faithful to it in spite of us and remains nearer to the eternal truth of life, which is full of snares and hostile forces.

But how much care and study are needed to succeed in fulfilling this duty! And how complicated it has become since the days of the silent caverns and the great deserted lakes! It was all so simple, then, so easy and so clear. The lonely hollow opened upon the side of the hill, and all that approached, all that moved on the horizon of the plains or woods, was the unmistakable enemy.... But to-day you can no longer tell.... You have to acquaint yourself with a civilization of which you disapprove, to appear to understand a thousand incomprehensible things.... Thus, it seems evident that henceforth the whole world no longer belongs to the master, that his property conforms to unintelligible limits.... It becomes necessary, therefore, first of all to know exactly where the sacred domain begins and ends. Whom are you to suffer, whom to stop?... There is the road by which every one, even the poor, has the right to pass. Why? You do not know; it is a fact which you deplore, but which you are bound to accept. Fortunately, on the other hand, here is the fair path which none may tread. This path is faithful to the sound traditions; it is not to be lost sight of; for by it enter into your daily existence the difficult problems of life.

Would you have an example? You are sleeping peacefully in a ray of the sun that covers the threshold of the kitchen with pearls. The earthenware pots are amusing themselves by elbowing and nudging one another on the edge of the shelves trimmed with paper lace-work. The copper stewpans play at scattering spots of light over the smooth white walls. The motherly stove hums a soft tune and dandles three saucepans blissfully dancing; and, from the little hole that lights up its inside, defies the good dog who cannot approach, by constantly putting out at him its fiery tongue. The clock, bored in its oak case, before striking the august hour of meal time, swings its great gilt navel to and fro; and the cunning flies tease your ears. On the glittering table lie a chicken, a hare, three partridges, besides other things which are called fruits—peaches, melons, grapes—and which are all good for nothing. The cook guts a big silver fish and throws the entrails (instead of giving them to you!) into the dust-bin. Ah, the dust-bin! Inexhaustible treasury, receptacle of windfalls, the jewel of the house! You shall have your share of it, an exquisite and surreptitious share; but it does not do to seem to know where it is. You are strictly forbidden to rummage in it. Man in this way prohibits many pleasant things, and life would be dull indeed and your days empty if you had to obey all the orders of the pantry, the cellar and the dining-room. Luckily, he is absent-minded and does not long remember the instructions which he lavishes. He is easily deceived. You achieve your ends and do as you please, provided you have the patience to await the hour. You are subject to man, and he is the one god; but you none the less have your own personal, exact and imperturbable morality, which proclaims aloud that illicit acts become most lawful through the very fact that they are performed without the master's knowledge. Therefore, let us close the watchful eye that has seen. Let us pretend to sleep and to dream of the moon....

Hark! A gentle tapping at the blue window that looks out on the garden! What is it? Nothing; a bough of hawthorn that has come to see what we are doing in the cool kitchen. Trees are inquisitive and often excited; but they do not count, one has nothing to say to them, they are irresponsible, they obey the wind, which has no princi-ples.... But what is that? I hear steps!... Up, ears open; nose on the alert!... It is the baker coming up to the rails, while the postman is opening a little gate in the hedge of lime-trees. They are friends; it is well; they bring something: you can greet them and wag your tail discreetly twice or thrice, with a patronizing smile....

Another alarm! What is it now? A carriage pulls up in front of the steps. The problem is a complex one. Before all, it is of consequence to heap copious insults on the horses, great, proud beasts, who make no reply. Meantime, you examine out of the corner of your eye the persons alighting. They are well-clad and seem full of confidence. They are probably going to sit at the table of the gods. The proper thing is to bark without acrimony, with a shade of respect, so as to show that you are doing your duty, but that you are doing it with intelligence. Nevertheless, you cherish a lurking suspicion and, behind the guests' backs, stealthily, you sniff the air persistently and in a knowing way, in order to discern any hidden intentions.

But halting footsteps resound outside the kitchen. This time it is the poor man dragging his crutch, the unmistakable enemy, the hereditary enemy, the direct descendant of him who roamed outside the bone-cramped cave which you suddenly see again in your racial memory. Drunk with indignation, your bark broken, your teeth multiplied with hatred and rage, you are about to seize their reconcilable adversary by the breeches, when the cook, armed with her broom, the ancillary and forsworn sceptre, comes to protect the traitor, and you are obliged to go back to your hole, where, with eyes filled with impotent and slanting flames, you growl out frightful, but futile curses, thinking within yourself that this is the end of all things, and that the human species has lost its notion of justice and injustice....

Is that all? Not yet; for the smallest life is made up of innumerous duties, and it is a long work to organize a happy existence upon the borderland of two such different worlds as the world of beasts and the world of men. How should we fare if we had to serve, while remaining within our own sphere, a divinity, not an imaginary one, like to ourselves, because the offspring of our own brain, but a god actually visible, ever present, ever active and as foreign, as superior to our being as we are to the dog?

We now, to return to Pelléas, know pretty well what to do and how to behave on the master's premises. But the world does not end at the house-door, and, beyond the walls and beyond the hedge, there is a universe of which one has not the custody, where one is no longer at home, where relations are changed. How are we to stand in the street, in the fields, in the market-place, in the shops? In consequence of difficult and delicate observations, we understand that we must take no notice of passers-by; obey no calls but the master's; be polite, with indifference, to strangers who pet us. Next, we must conscientiously fulfil certain obligations of mysterious courtesy toward our brothers the other dogs; respect chickens and ducks; not appear to remark the cakes at the pastry-cook's, which spread themselves insolently within reach of the tongue; show to the cats, who, on the steps of the houses, provoke us by hideous grimaces, a silent contempt, but one that will not forget; and remember that it is lawful and even commendable to chase and strangle mice, rats, wild rabbits and, generally speaking, all animals (we learn to know them by secret marks) that have not yet made their peace with mankind.

All this and so much more!... Was it surprising that Pelléas often appeared pensive in the face of those numberless problems, and that his humble and gentle look was often so profound and grave, laden with cares and full of unreadable questions?

Alas, he did not have time to finish the long and heavy task which nature lays upon the instinct that rises in order to approach a brighter region.... An ill of a mysterious character, which seems specially to punish the only animal that succeeds in leaving the circle in which it is born; an indefinite ill that carries off hundreds of intelligent little dogs, came to put an end to the destiny and the happy education of Pelléas. And now all those efforts to achieve a little more light; all that ardour in loving, that courage in under-standing; all that affectionate gaiety and innocent fawning; all those kind and devoted looks, which turned to man to ask for his assistance against unjust death; all those flickering gleams which came from the profound abyss of a world that is no longer ours; all those nearly human little habits lie sadly in the cold ground, under a flowering elder-tree, in a corner of the garden.

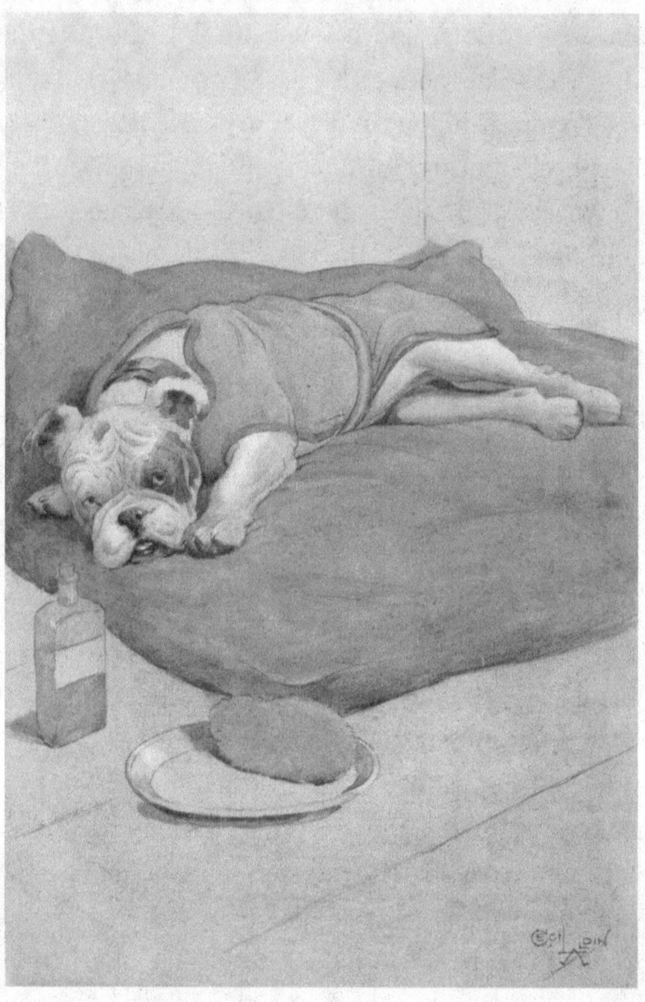

II

Man loves the dog, but how much more ought he to love it if he considered, in the inflexible harmony of the laws of nature, the sole exception, which is that love of a being that succeeds in piercing, in order to draw closer to us, the partitions, every elsewhere impermeable, that separate the species! We are alone, absolutely alone on this chance planet; and amid all the forms of life that surround us, not one, excepting the dog, has made an alliance with us. A few creatures fear us, most are unaware of us, and not one loves us. In the world of plants, we have dumb and motionless slaves; but they serve us in spite of themselves. They simply endure our laws and our yoke. They are impotent prisoners, victims incapable of escaping, but silently rebellious; and, so soon as we lose sight of them, they hasten to betray us and return to their former wild and mischievous liberty. The rose and the corn, had they wings, would fly at our approach like the birds.

Among the animals, we number a few servants who have submitted only through indifference, cowardice or stupidity: the uncertain and craven horse, who responds only to pain and is attached to nothing; the passive and dejected ass, who stays with us only because he knows not what to do nor where to go, but who nevertheless, under the cudgel and the pack-saddle, retains the idea that lurks behind his ears; the cow and the ox, happy so long as they are eating, and docile because, for centuries, they have not had a thought of their own; the affrighted sheep, who knows no other master than terror; the hen, who is faithful to the poultry-yard because she finds more maize and wheat there than in the neighbouring forest. I do not speak of the cat, to whom we are nothing more than a too large and uneatable prey: the ferocious cat, whose sidelong contempt tolerates us only as encumbering parasites in our own homes. She, at least, curses us in her mysterious heart; but all the others live beside us as they might live beside a rock or a tree. They do not love us, do not know us, scarcely notice us. They are unaware of our life, our death, our departure, our return, our sadness, our joy, our smile. They do not even hear the sound of our voice, so soon as it no longer threatens them; and, when they look at us, it is with the distrustful bewilderment of the horse, in whose eye still hovers the infatuation of the elk or gazelle that sees us for the first time, or with the dull stupor of the ruminants, who look upon us as a momentary and useless accident of the pasture.

For thousands of years, they have been living at our side, as foreign to our thoughts, our affections, our habits as though the least fraternal of the stars had dropped them but yesterday on our globe. In the boundless interval that separates man from all the other creatures, we have succeeded only, by dint of patience, in making them take two or three illusory steps. And if, to-morrow, leaving their feelings toward us untouched, nature were to give them the intelligence and the weapons wherewith to conquer us, I confess that I should distrust the hasty vengeance of the horse, the obstinate reprisals of the ass and the maddened meekness of the sheep. I should shun the cat as I should shun the tiger; and even the good cow, solemn and somnolent, would inspire me with but a wary confidence. As for the hen, with her round, quick eye, as when discovering a slug or a worm, I am sure that she would devour me without a thought.

III

Now, in this indifference and this total want of comprehension in which everything that surrounds us lives; in this incommunicable world, where everything has its object hermetically contained within itself, where every destiny is self-circumscribed, where there exist among the creatures no other relations than those of executioners and victims, eaters and eaten, where nothing is able to leave its steel-bound sphere, where death alone establishes cruel relations of cause and effect between neighbouring lives, where not the smallest sympathy has ever made a conscious leap from one species to another, one animal alone, among all that breathes upon the earth, has succeeded in breaking through the prophetic circle, in escaping from itself to come bounding toward us, definitely to cross the enormous zone of darkness, ice and silence that isolates each category of existence in nature's unintelligible plan. This animal, our good familiar dog, simple and unsurprising as may to-day appear to us what he has done, in thus perceptibly drawing nearer to a world in which he was not born and for which he was not destined, has nevertheless performed one of the most unusual and improbable acts that we can find in the general history of life. When was this recognition of man by beast, this extraordinary passage from darkness to light, effected? Did we seek out the poodle, the collie, or the mastiff from among the wolves and the jackals, or did he come spontaneously to us? We cannot tell. So far as our human annals stretch, he is at our side, as at present; but what are human annals in comparison with the times of which we have no witness? The fact remains that he is there in our houses, as ancient, as rightly placed, as perfectly adapted to our habits as though he had appeared on this earth, such as he now is, at the same time as ourselves. We have not to gain his confidence or his friendship: he is born our friend; while his eyes are still closed, already he believes in us: even before his birth, he has given himself to man. But the word "friend" does not exactly depict his affectionate worship. He loves us and reveres us as though we had drawn him out of nothing. He is, before all, our creature full of gratitude and more devoted than the apple of our eye. He is our intimate and impassioned slave, whom nothing discourages, whom nothing repels, whose ardent trust and love nothing can impair. He has solved, in an admirable and touching manner, the terrifying problem which human wisdom would have to solve if a divine race came to occupy our globe. He has loyally, religiously, irrevocably recognized man's superiority and has surrendered himself to him body and soul, without after-thought, without any intention to go back, reserving of his independence, his instinct and his character only the small part indispensable to the continuation of the life prescribed by nature. With an unquestioning certainty, an unconstraint and a simplicity that surprise us a little, deeming us better and more powerful than all that exists, he betrays, for our benefit, the whole of the animal kingdom to which he belongs and, without scruple, denies his race, his kin, his mother and his young.

But he loves us not only in his consciousness and his intelligence: the very instinct of his race, the entire unconsciousness of his species, it appears, think only of us, dream only of being useful to us. To serve us better, to adapt himself better to our different needs, he has adopted every shape and been able infinitely to vary the faculties, the aptitudes which he places at our disposal. Is he to aid us in the pursuit of game in the plains? His legs lengthen inordinately, his muzzle tapers, his lungs widen, he becomes swifter than the deer. Does our prey hide under wood? The docile genius of the species, forestalling our desires, presents us with the basset, a sort of almost footless serpent, which steals into the closest thickets. Do we ask that he should drive our flocks? The same compliant genius grants him the requisite size, intelligence, energy and vigilance. Do we intend him to watch and defend our house? His head becomes round and monstrous, in order that his jaws may be more powerful, more formidable and more tenacious. Are we taking him to the south? His hair grows shorter and lighter, so that he may faithfully accompany us under the rays of a hotter sun. Are we going up to the north? His feet grow larger, the better to tread the snow; his fur thickens, in order that the cold may not compel him to abandon us. Is he intended only for us to play with, to amuse the leisure of our eyes, to adorn or enliven the home? He clothes himself in a sovereign grace and elegance, he makes himself smaller than a doll to sleep on our knees by the fireside, or even consents, should our fancy demand it, to appear a little ridiculous to please us.

You shall not find, in nature's immense crucible, a single living being that has shown a like suppleness, a similar abundance of forms, the same prodigious faculty of accommodation to our wishes. This is because, in the world which we know, among the different and primitive geniuses that preside over the evolution of the several species, there exists not one, excepting that of the dog, that ever gave a thought to the presence of man.

It will, perhaps, be said that we have been able to transform almost as profoundly some of our domestic animals: our hens, our pigeons, our ducks, our cats, our horses, our rabbits, for instance. Yes, perhaps; although such transformations are not comparable with those undergone by the dog and although the kind of service which these animals render us remains, so to speak, invariable. In any case, whether this impression be purely imaginary or correspond with a reality, it does not appear that we feel in these transformations the same unfailing and preventing good will, the same sagacious and exclusive love. For the rest, it is quite possible that the dog, or rather the inaccessible genius of his race, troubles scarcely at all about us and that we have merely known how to make use of various aptitudes offered by the abundant chances of life. It matters not: as we know nothing of the substance of things, we must needs cling to appearances; and it is sweet to establish that, at least in appearance, there is on the planet where, like unacknowledged kings, we live in solitary state, a being that loves us.

However the case may stand with these appearances, it is none the less certain that, in the aggregate of intelligent creatures that have rights, duties, a mission and a destiny, the dog is a really privileged animal. He occupies in this world a pre-eminent position enviable among all. He is the only living being that has found and recognizes an indubitable, tangible, unexceptionable and definite god. He knows to what to devote the best part of himself. He knows to whom above him to give himself. He has not to seek for a perfect, superior and infinite power in the darkness, amid successive lies, hypotheses and dreams. That power is there, before him, and he moves in its light. He knows the supreme duties which we all do not know. He has a morality which surpasses all that he is able to discover in himself and which he can practise without scruple and without fear. He possesses truth in its fulness. He has a certain and infinite ideal.

IV

And it was thus that, the other day, before his illness, I saw my little Pelléas sitting at the foot of my writing-table, his tail carefully folded under his paws, his head a little on one side, the better to question me, at once attentive and tranquil, as a saint should be in the presence of God. He was happy with the happiness which we, perhaps, shall never know, since it sprang from the smile and the approval of a life incomparably higher than his own. He was there, studying, drinking in all my looks; and he replied to them gravely, as from equal to equal, to inform me, no doubt, that, at least through the eyes the most immaterial organ that transformed into affectionate intelligence the light which we enjoyed, he knew that he was saying to me all that love should say. And, when I saw him thus, young, ardent and believing, bringing me, in some wise, from the depths of unwearied nature, quite fresh news of life and trusting and wonderstruck, as though he had been the first of his race that came to inaugurate the earth and as though we were still in the first days of the world's existence, I envied the gladness of his certainty, compared it with the destiny of man, still plunging on every side into darkness, and said to myself that the dog who meets with a good master is the happier of the two.

THE TEMPLE OF CHANCE

TRANSLATED BY ALEXANDER TEIXEIRA DE MATTOS.

I

I sacrificed—for it is a sacrifice to forsake the incomparable play of the stars and moon on the divine Mediterranean—I sacrificed a few evenings of my stay in the land of the sun to the consulting of the most mystic god of this world of ours in the busiest, the most gorgeous and the most individual of his temples.

This temple stands down there, at Monte Carlo, on a rock bathed in the dazzling light of the sea and sky. Enchanted gardens, where blossom in January all the flowers of spring, summer and autumn, sweet-scented thickets that borrow nothing from the hostile seasons but their perfume and their smiles lie before its porch. The orange, most lovable of all trees, the palm, the lemon-tree, the mimosa wreathe it with gaiety. The crowds approach it by royal stairways. But, mark you, the building is not worthy of the admirable site which it commands, of the delicious hills, the azure and emerald gulf, the happy meadows that surround it. Nor is it worthy either of the god whom it shelters or of the idea which it represents. It is insipidly emphatic and hideously blatant. It suggests the low insolence, the overweening conceit of the flunkey who has grown rich but remains obsequious. Examination shows it to be solidly built and very large; nevertheless, it wears the mean and sadly pretentious air of the ephemeral palaces of our great exhibitions. The august father of Destiny has been housed in a sort of meringue covered with preserved fruits and sugar castles. Perhaps the residence was purposely made ridiculous. The builders may have feared lest they should warn or alarm the crowd. They probably wished to make it believe that the kindliest, the most frivolous, the most harmlessly capricious, the least serious of the gods awaited his worshippers on a throne of cakes inside this confectioner's master-piece. Ah, no; a mysterious and grave divinity reigns here, a wise and sovereign force, harmonious and sure. He should have been throned in a bare marble palace, severe, simple and colossal, high and vast, cold and spiritual, rectangular and rigid, positive and overwhelming.

II

The interior corresponds with the exterior. The rooms are spacious, but decorated with hackneyed magnificence. The acolytes of Chance, the bored, indifferent, monotonous croupiers, look like shop-assistants in their Sunday clothes. They are not the high-priests, but the office-clerks of Hazard. The rites and implements of the cult are vulgar and commonplace: a few tables, some chairs; here, a sort of bowl or cylinder that turns in the centre of each table, with a tiny ivory ball that rolls in the opposite direction; there, a few packs of cards; and that is all. It needs no more to evoke the immeasurable power that holds the stars in suspense.

III

Around the tables crowd the faithful. Each of them carries within himself hopes, belief, different and invisible tragedies and comedies. This, I think, is the spot in which more nervous force and more human passions are accumulated and absolutely squandered than in any other in the world. This is the ill-omened spot where the peerless and, perhaps, divine substance of substances, which, in every other place, works pregnant miracles, prodigies of strength, of beauty and of love, this is the fatal spot where the flower of the soul, the most precious fluid on the planet, leaks away into nothingness!... No more criminal waste can be conceived. This unprofitable force, which knows neither whither to go nor what work to do, which finds no door nor window, no direct object nor manner of transmission, hovers over the table like a mortal shadow, falls back upon itself and creates a particular atmosphere, a sort of sweating silence which somehow suggests the fever of true silence. In this unwholesome stillness, the voice of Fate's little book-keeper snuffles out the sacred formula:

"Faites vos jeux, messieurs, faites vos jeux!"

That is to say, make to the hidden god the sacrifice which he demands before he shows himself. Then, somewhere from the crowd, a hand bright with certainty places imperiously the fruit of a year's work on numbers that cannot fail. Other adorers, more cunning, more circumspect, less confident, compound with luck, distribute their chances, compute illusive probabilities and, having studied the mood and peculiarities of the genius of the table, lay complex and knowing traps for it. Others, again, hand over a considerable portion of their happiness or their life, at random, to the caprice of numbers.

But now the second formula resounds:

"Rien ne va plus!"

That is to say, the god is about to speak! At this moment, an eye that could pierce the easy veil of appearances would distinctly see scattered on the plain green cloth (if not actually, then at least potentially; for a single stake is rare, and he who plays of his superfluity to-day will risk his all to-morrow) a corn-field ripening in the sun a thousand miles away; or, again, in other squares, a meadow, a wood, a moonlit country-house, a shop in some little market-town, a staff of book-keepers and accountants bending over ledgers in their gloomy offices, peasants labouring in the rain, hundreds of work-girls slaving from morn to night in deadly factories, miners in the mines, sailors on their ship; the jewels of debauchery, love or glory; a prison, a dockyard; joy, misery, injustice, cruelty, avarice; crimes, privations, tears. All this lies there, very peacefully, in those little heaps of smiling gold, in those flimsy scraps of paper which ordain disasters which even a life-time would be powerless ever to efface. The slightest timid and hesitating movements of these yellow counters and blue notes will rebound and swell out in the distance, in the real world, in the streets, in the plains, in the trees, in men's blood and in their hearts. They will demolish the house that saw the parents die, carry off the old man's chair, give a new squire to the astonished village, close a workshop, take away the bread from the children of a hamlet, divert the course of a river, stay or break a life and, through an infinity of time and space, burst the links of an uninterrupted chain of cause and effect. But none of these resounding truths utters an indiscreet whisper here. There are here more sleeping Furies than on the purple steps of the palace of the Atridæ; but their cries of waking and of pain lie hidden at the bottom of men's hearts. Nothing betrays, nothing foretells that there are definite ills hovering over those present and choosing their victims. Only, the eyes stare a little, while hands shiftily finger a pencil, a bit of paper. Not an unaccustomed word or gesture. Clammy expectation sits motionless. For this is the place of voiceless pantomime, of stifled fighting, of unblinking despair, of tragedy masked in silence, of dumb destiny sinking in an atmosphere of lies that swallows up every sound.

IV

Meanwhile, the little ball spins on the cylinder, and I reflect upon all that is destroyed by the formidable power conferred on it through a monstrous compact. Each time that it thus starts in search of the mysterious answer, it annihilates all around it the last essential remnants of our social morality: I mean, the value of money. To abolish the value of money and substitute for it a higher ideal would be an admirable achievement; but to abolish it and leave in its place simply nothing is, I conceive, one of the gravest crimes that can be committed against our scheme of evolution. If we look at it from a certain point of view and purify it of its incidental vices, money is essentially a very worthy symbol: it represents human effort and labour; it is, for the most part, the fruit of laudable sacrifice and noble toil. Whereas here, this symbol, one of the last that was left to us, is daily subjected to public mockery. Suddenly, at the caprice of a little thing as insignificant as a child's toy, ten years of striving, of conscientious thought, of tasks patiently endured lose all importance. If this hideous phenomenon were not isolated on this one rock, no social organization but would have fallen victim to the injury spreading from it. Even now, in its leprous isolation, this devastating influence makes itself felt at a distance that never could have been estimated. We feel that this influence, so inevitable, so malevolent and so profound, is such that, when we leave this cursed palace where gold clinks incessantly against the human conscience, we wonder how it is that the everyday life goes on, that patient gardeners consent to keep up the flower-beds in front of the fatal building, that wretched guardians can be found to watch over its precincts for a contemptible wage and that a poor little old woman, at the bottom of its marble stairs, amid the coming and going of lucky or ruined gamblers, for years persists in earning a laborious livelihood by selling pennyworths of oranges, almonds, nuts and matches to the passers-by.

V

While we are making these reflections, the ivory ball slackens its course and begins to hop like a noisy insect over the thirty-seven compartments that allure it. This is the irrevocable judgment. O strange infirmity of our eyes, our ears and that brain of which we are so proud! O strange secrets of the most elementary laws of this world! From the second at which the ball was set in motion to the second at which it falls into the fateful hole, on the battle-field three yards long, in this childish and mocking form, the mystery of the Universe inflicts a symbolical, incessant and disheartening defeat upon human power and reason. Collect around this table all the wise men, all the divines, all the seers, all the sages, all the prophets, all the saints, all the wonder-workers, all the mathematicians, all the geniuses of every time and every country; ask them to search their reason, their soul, their knowledge, their Heaven for the number so close at hand, the number already almost part of the present at which the little ball will end its race; beg them, so that they may foretell that number to us, to invoke their gods that know all, their thoughts that govern the nations and aspire to penetrate the worlds: all their efforts will break against this brief puzzle which a child could take in its hand and which no longer fills the smallest moment's space. No one has been able to do it, no one will ever do it. And all the strength, all the certainty of the "bank," which is the impassive, stubborn, determined and ever-victorious ally of the rhythmical and absolute wisdom of Chance, lies solely in the establishment of man's powerlessness to foresee, were it but for the third of a second, that which is about to happen before his eyes. If, in the span of nearly fifty years during which these formidable experiments have been made on this flower-clad rock, one single being had been found who, in the course of an afternoon, had torn the veil of mystery that covers, at each throw, the tiny future of the tiny ball, the bank would have been broken, the undertaking wrecked. But that abnormal being has not appeared; and the bank well knows that he will never come to sit at one of its tables. We see, therefore, how, in spite of all his pride and all his hopes, man knows that he can know nothing.

VI

In truth, Chance, in the sense in which the gamblers understand it, is a god without existence. They worship only a lie, which each of them pictures to himself in a different shape. Each of them ascribes to it laws, habits, preferences that are utterly contradictory, as a whole, and purely imaginary. According to some, it favours certain numbers. According to others, it obeys certain rhythms that are easily grasped. According to others again, it contains within itself a sort of justice that ends by giving an equal value to each group of chances. According to others, lastly, it cannot possibly favour indefinitely any particular series of simple chances for the benefit of the bank. We should never come to an end if we tried to review the whole illusory *corpus juris* of roulette. It is true that, in practice, the indefinite repetition of the same limited accidents necessarily forms groups of coincidences in which the gambler's deluded eye seems to discern some phantom laws. But it is no less true that, upon trial, at the moment when you rely upon the assistance of the surest phantom, it vanishes abruptly and leaves you face to face with the unknown which it was masking. For the rest, most gamblers bring to the green cloth many other illusions, conscious or instinctive, and infinitely less justifiable. Almost all persuade themselves that Chance reserves for them special and premeditated favours or misfortunes. Almost all imagine some undefined but plausible connection to exist between the little ivory sphere and their presence, their passions, their desires, their vices, their virtues, their merits, their intellectual or moral power, their beauty, their genius, the enigma of their being, their future, their happiness and their life. Is it necessary to say that there is no such connection; that there could be none? That little sphere whose judgment they implore, upon which they hope to exercise an occult influence, that incorruptible little ball has something else to do than to occupy itself with their joys and sorrows. It has but thirty or forty seconds of movement and of life; and, during those thirty or forty seconds, it has to obey more eternal rules, to resolve more infinite problems, to accomplish more essential duties than would ever find place in man's consciousness or comprehension. It has, among other enormous and difficult things, to reconcile in its brief course those two incomprehensible and immeasurable powers which are probably the biform soul of the Universe: centrifugal force and centripetal force. It has to reckon with all the laws of gravitation, friction, the resistance of the air, all the phenomena of matter. It has to pay attention to the smallest incidents of the earth or sky; for a gambler who leaves his seat and imperceptibly disturbs the floor of the room, or a star that rises in the firmament, compels it to modify and begin anew the whole of its mathematical operations. It has no time to play the part of a goddess either well or ill-disposed towards mortals; it is forbidden to neglect a single one of the numberless formalities which infinity demands of all that moves within it. And, when, at last, it attains its goal, it has performed the same incalculable work as the moon or the other cold and indifferent planets that, outside, above, in the transparent azure, rise majestically over the sapphire and silver waters of the Mediterranean. This long work we call Chance, having no other name to give to that which we do not as yet understand.

IN PRAISE OF THE SWORD!

TRANSLATED BY ALEXANDER TEIXEIRA DE MATTOS.

I

Man, greedy of justice, tries in a thousand various manners, often empirical, sometimes wise, whimsical at other times and superstitious, to conjure up the shade of the great goddess necessary to his existence. A strange, elusive and yet most living goddess! An immaterial divinity that cannot stand upright save in our secret heart; one of which we may say that, the more visible temples that it has, the less real power it possesses. A day will break, perhaps, when it shall have no other palaces than our several consciences; and, on that day, it will reign really in the silence that is the sacred element of its life. In the meanwhile, we multiply the organs through which we hope that it will make itself heard. We lend it human and solemn voices; and when it is silent in others and even in ourselves, we proceed to question it beyond our own conscience, on the uncertain confines of our being, where we become a part of chance and where we believe that justice blends with God and our own destiny.

II

It is this insatiable need which, on those points where human justice remained dumb and declared itself powerless, appealed in former days to the judgment of God. To-day, when the idea which we have conceived of the divinity has changed its form and nature, the same instinct persists, so deep, so general, that it is perhaps but the half-transparent veil of an approaching truth. If we no longer look to God to approve or condemn that which men are unable to judge, we now confide that mission to the unconscious, incognizable and, so to speak, future part of ourselves. The duel invokes no longer the judgment of God, but that of our future, our luck or our destiny, composed of all that is indefinite within us. It is called upon, in the name of our good or evil possibilities, to declare whether, from the point of view of inexplicable life, we are wrong or right.

There we have the indelibly human thing that is disengaged from amid all the absurdities and puerilities of our present encounters. However unreasonable it may appear, this sort of supreme interrogation, this question put in the night which is no longer illumined by intelligible justice, can hardly be waived so long as we have not found a less equivocal manner of weighing the rights and wrongs, the essential hopes and inequalities of two destinies that wish to confront each other.

III

For the rest, to descend to the practical point of view from these regions haunted by more or less dangerous phantoms, it is certain that the duel, that is to say the possibility of securing justice for one's self outside the law and yet according to rule, responds to a need of which we cannot deny the existence. For we live in the midst of a society that does not protect us enough to deprive us, in all circumstances, of the right dearest to man's instinct.

It is unnecessary, I think, to enumerate the cases in which the protection afforded by society is insufficient. It would take less long to name those in which it suffices. Doubtless, for men who are lawfully weak and defenceless, it would be desirable that things were different; but for those who are capable of defending themselves it is most salutary that things should be as they are, for nothing suppresses initiative and personal character so greatly as does a too-zealous and too-constant protection. Remember that, before all, we are beings of prey and strife; that we must be careful not completely to extinguish within ourselves the qualities of primitive man, for it was not without reason that nature placed them there. If it is wise to restrain their excess, it is prudent to preserve their principle. We do not know the offensive tricks which the elements or the other forces of the universe have in store for us; and woe be to us, in all likelihood, if one day they find us entirely devoid of the spirit of vengeance, mistrust, anger, brutality, combativeness, and of many other faults, which are all very blameworthy from the human point of view, but which, far more than the most loudly-extolled abstemious virtues, have helped us to conquer the great enemies of our kind.

IV

It behoves us, therefore, in general, to praise those who do not allow themselves to be offended with impunity. They keep up among us an idea of extra-legal justice by which we all profit and which would soon become exhausted without their aid. Let us rather deplore that they are not more numerous. If there were not quite so many good-natured souls, capable of chastising, but too ready to forgive, we should find far fewer evil-doers too ready to do wrong; for three-quarters of the wrong that is committed springs from the certainty of impunity. In order to maintain the vague fear and respect that allow the unfortunate unarmed to live and breathe almost freely in a society teeming with knaves and dastards, it is the strict duty of all who are able to resist unpunishable injustice by means of an act of violence never fail to do so. They thus restore the level of immanent justice. Thinking that they are defending only themselves, they defend in the aggregate the most precious heritage of mankind. I do not contend that it would not be better, in the greater number of cases, that the courts should intervene; but, until our laws become simpler, more practical, less costly and more familiar, we have no other remedy than the fist or the sword against a number of iniquities that are very real, although not provided for by our codes.

V

The fist is quick, immediate; but it is not conclusive enough; when the offence is at all grave, we see that it is really too lenient and ephemeral; and, besides, it has always movements that are a little vulgar and effects that are somewhat repugnant. It brings only a brutal faculty into play. It is the blindest and most unequal of weapons; and, since it evades all the conditions that adjust the chances of two ill-matched adversaries, it involves exaggerated reprisals on the part of the beaten combatant, which end by arming him with the stick, the knife or the revolver.

It is allowable in certain countries, in England, for instance. There the science of boxing forms part of the elementary education and its general practice tends in a curious way to remove natural inequalities; moreover, a whole organism of clubs, paternal juries and tribunals easy of access confirms or forestalls its exploits. But in France it would be a pity to return to it. The sword, which has there replaced it since immemorial days, is an incomparably more sensitive, serious, graceful and delicate instrument of justice. It is reproached with being neither equitable nor probative. But it proves first of all the quality of our attitude in the face of danger; and that already is a proof which is not without its value. For our attitude in the face of danger is exactly our attitude in the face of the reproaches or encouragements of the various consciences that lie hidden within us, of those which are both below and above our intelligible conscience and which mingle with the essential and, so to speak, universal elements of our being. Next, it depends only upon ourselves that it should become as equitable as any human instrument, ever subject to chance, error and weakness, can be. Its art is certainly accessible to every healthy man. It demands neither abnormal muscular strength nor exceptional agility. The least gifted of us need devote to it no more than two or three hours of every week. He will acquire a suppleness and a precision sufficient soon to discover what the astronomers call his "personal equation," to attain his individual average, which is at the same time a general average that only a few fire-eaters, a few idlers succeed in surpassing, at the cost of long, painful and very ungrateful efforts.

VI

Having attained this average, we can entrust our lives to the point of the frail but formidable sword. It is the magician that at once establishes new relations between two forces which none would have dreamt of comparing. It allows the pigmy who is in the right to confront the colossus who is in the wrong. It gracefully leads enormous violence, horned like the bull, to lighter and brighter summits; and behold, the primitive animal is obliged to stand still before a power that has nothing left in common with the mean, shapeless, tyrannical virtues of earth: I mean weight, mass, quantity, the stupid cohesion of matter. Between the sword and the fist lie the breadth of a universe, an ocean of centuries and almost as great a distance as separates beast from man. The sword is iron and wit, steel and intelligence. It makes the muscles subservient to thought and compels thought to respect the muscles that serve it. It is ideal and practical, chimerical and full of good sense. It is dazzling and clear as lightning, insinuating, elusive and multiform as a ray of the sun or moon. It is faithful and capricious, nobly guileful, loyally false. It decks rancour and hatred with a smile. It transfigures brutality. Thanks to the sword, reason, courage, rightful assurance, patience, contempt of danger, man's sacrifice to love, to an idea, a whole moral world, in short, as by a fairy bridge swung over the abyss of darkness, enters as the master into the original chaos, reduces and organizes it. The sword is man's pre-eminent weapon, that weapon which, were all the others tried and itself unknown, would have to be invented, because it best serves his most various, his most purely human faculties and because it is the most direct, the most tractable and the most loyal instrument of his defensive intelligence, strength and justice.

VII

But what is most admirable is that its decisions are not mechanical nor mathematically pre-established. In this it resembles those pastimes in which chance and knowledge are marvellously mingled in order to question our fortune: pastimes almost mystical and always enthralling, in which man delights to sound his luck on the confines of his existence.

Bring face to face two adversaries of manifestly unequal powers: it is not inevitable, it is not even certain that the more vigorous and the more skilful will gain the day over the other. Once that we have conquered our personal mastership, our sword becomes ourself, with our qualities and our defects. It is our firmness, our devotion, our will, our daring, our conviction, our justice, our hesitation, our impatience, our fear. We have cultivated it with care. We have risen to the height of the possibilities which it was able to offer us. We have given it all that we were able to dispose of; it restores to us integrally all that we entrusted to it. We have nothing wherewith to reproach ourselves; we are in accord with the instinct and duty of self-preservation. But the sword represents something more, and exactly that part of us which we are compelled to risk at the graver moments of existence. It personifies an unknown portion of our being and personifies it in the most favourable and solemn conjuncture that man can imagine wherein to call upon his destiny, that is to say, in circumstances in which the mysterious entity that lives within him is directly seconded by all the faculties subjected to his consciousness.

It thus brings face to face not only two forces, two intelligences and two liberties, but also two chances, two fortunes, two mysteries, two destinies, which, over and above the rest, like the gods of Homer, preside over the combat, run, flash, dart and meet upon its blade. When it seems to be striking before us in space, it is really knocking at the doors of our fate; and, while death hovers around it, he who handles it feels that it is escaping from its previous bondage and suddenly obeying other laws than those which used to guide it in the fencing-school. It fulfils a secret mission; before pronouncing sentence, it judges us; or rather, by the mere fact that we are wielding it distractedly in the presence of the great and formidable enigma, it forces our destiny to judge ourselves.

DEATH AND THE CROWN

TRANSLATED BY ALEXANDER TEIXEIRA DE MATTOS.

I

The months of June and July of the year 1902 set for the meditation of men one of those tragic spectacles which, to speak truly, we encounter every day in the little life that surrounds us, although, like so many great things, they there pass unperceived. They do not assume their full significance, nor finally capture our gaze, except when performed on one of those enormous stages on which are heaped, so to speak, all the thoughts of a people and on which the latter loves to behold its own existence made greater and more solemn by royal actors.

As is said in a modern play, "We must add something to ordinary life before we can understand it." Fate added, in this case, the power and the pomp of one of the most glorious thrones on earth. Thanks to the resplendency of that pomp and that power, we saw exactly what a man is in himself and what he remains when the imposing laws of nature strip him cruelly naked before their tribunal. We learnt also—the force of love, pity, religion and science having been suddenly exerted to the utmost—we learnt also to know better the value of the aid which all that we have acquired since we inhabited this planet can give in our distress. We assisted at a struggle, ever confused, but as fierce as though it were doomed to be supreme, between the different powers, physical and moral, visible and invisible, that to-day guide mankind.

II

Edward VII. King of England, the illustrious victim of a whim of fate, lay pitifully hovering between the crown and death. This fate, with one hand, held to his brow one of the most magnificent diadems that the revolutions have spared; and, with the other, it forced that same brow, moist with the sweat of the death-agony, to bend down towards a wide-open tomb. In sinister fashion, it prolonged this game for more than two months.

If we contemplate the event from a point a little higher than the elevation of the humble hills on which life's numberless anecdotes unfold themselves, it is here not only a question of the tragedy of an opulent monarch stricken by nature at the very moment when thousands of men are aspiring to place some small portion of their hopes and of their fairest dreams in his person, beyond the reach of destiny and above humanity. Neither is it a question of appreciating the irony of that moment in which they would assert and establish something supernatural that declined upon something most normally natural; something that should be contradictory to the pitiless levelling laws of the indifferent planet which we all inhabit with a sort of heedless tolerance; something that should reassure them and console them as an admirable exception to their misery and frailty. No, it is here a question of the essential tragedy of man, of the universal and perpetual drama enacted between his feeble will and the enormous unknown force that encompasses him, between the little flame of his mind or soul, that inexplicable phenomenon of nature, and vast matter, that other, equally inexplicable, phenomenon of the same nature. This drama, with its thousand undetermined catastrophes, has not ceased to unfold itself for a single day since a portion of blind and colossal life conceived the somewhat strange idea of taking in us a sort of consciousness of itself. This time, a more resplendent accident than the others came to display the drama on a loftier height, which was illumined for an instant by all the longings, all the wishes, all the fears, all the uncertainties, all the prayers, all the doubts, all the illusions, all the wills, all the looks, lastly, of the inhabitants of our globe hastening in thought to the foot of the solemn mountain.

III

Slowly, then, it unfolded itself up there; and we were able to compute our resources. We had the opportunity to weigh in luminous scales our illusions and our realities. All the confidence and all the wretchedness of our kind were symbolically concentrated in a single hour and in a single being. Would it be proved once more that the longings, the most ardent wishes, the will and the most imperious love of a prodigious assembly of men are powerless to cause the most insignificant of physical laws to swerve by one line's breadth? Would it be established once more that, when standing in the face of nature, we must seek our defensive laws not in the moral or sentimental, but in another world? It is salutary therefore to look at that which happened upon that summit firmly and with an eye that no longer attributes things to spells.

IV

Some beheld in it the mighty manifestation of a jealous and all-powerful God, Who holds us in His hand and laughs at our poor glory; the scornful gesture of a Providence too long neglected and incensed because man does not recognize with greater docility Its hidden existence nor fathom more easily Its enigmatic will. Were they mistaken? And who are they that are never mistaken in the darkness that is over us? But why does this God, more perfect than men, ask of us what a perfect man would not ask? Why does He make a too willing, an almost blindly accepted faith the first, the most necessary and indeed the only virtue? If He is incensed because He is not understood, because He is disobeyed, would it not be just that He should manifest Himself in such a manner that human reason, which He Himself created with its admirable demands, should not have to surrender the most precious, the most essential of its privileges in order to approach His throne? Now was this gesture, like so many others, clear enough, significant enough to force reason to its knees? And yet, if He loves that man should adore Him, as those who speak in His name proclaim, it would be easy for Him to constrain us all to adore Him alone. We only await an unexceptionable sign. In the name of that direct reflection of His light which He has set at the topmost point of our being, where burns, with an ardour, with a purity that grow fairer day by day, the single passion for certainty and truth, does it not seem that we have a right to it?

V

Others contemplated this King gasping for breath on the steps of the most splendid throne that still remains standing, this almost infinite power, shattered, broken, a prey to the dreadful enemies that assail suffering flesh, flesh destroyed under the most dazzling crown that the invisible and mocking hand of chance has ever suspended over a confused heap of anguish and distress....

They saw in it a new and terrifying proof of wretchedness, of human uselessness. They went about repeating to themselves what the wisdom of antiquity had already so well said, to wit that we are, that we probably always shall be, despite all our efforts, "but a grain in the proportion of substance and but the turning of a wimble in respect of time." Unbelieving in God, but believing in His shadow, they discovered in this, perhaps, a mysterious decree of that mysterious Justice which sometimes comes to place a little order in the shapeless history of men and to take vengeance on the kings for the iniquity of the nations....

They found in it many other things besides. They were not mistaken; all those things were there, because they are in ourselves and because the sense that we give to the incomprehensible actions of unknown forces soon becomes the sole human reality and peoples with more or less fraternal spectres the indifference and the nothingness that surround us.

VI

As for us, without rejecting those seductive or terrible spectres, which perhaps represent interventions of which our instinct has a presentiment, though our senses do not perceive them, let us, before all, fix our eyes on the really human and certain parts of that great accomplished drama. In the centre of the obscure cloud wherein were amplified, until they exceeded the confines of this terrestrial world, the acts of the power that, turn by turn, brought nearer and separated a solemn death and an illusive crown, we distinguish a man who is at last about to attain the sole object, the essential moment of his life. Suddenly, an unseen enemy attacks him and lays him low. Forthwith, other men run up. They are the princes of Science. They do not ask if it be God, Destiny, Chance, Justice that comes to obstruct the road of the victim whom they raise. Believers or unbelievers in other spheres or at other moments, they put no questions to the murky cloud. They are here the qualified envoys of the reason of our kind, of naked reason, abandoned to itself as it wanders alone in a monstrous universe. Deliberately, they cast off from it sentiment, imagination, all that does not properly belong to it. They use only the purely human, almost animal portion of its flame, as though they had the certainty that every being can vanquish a force of nature only by the, so to speak, specific force which nature has set within him. Thus handled, this flame is perhaps narrow and weak, but precise, exclusive, invincible as that of the blow-pipe of the enameller or the chemist. It is fed with facts, with minute, but sure and innumerable observations. It lights only insignificant and successive points in the immense unknown; but it does not stray, it goes where it is directed by the keen eye that guides it, and the point which it reaches is screened from the influences once called supernatural. Humbly it interrupts or diverts the order pre-established by nature. Scarce two or three years ago, it would have been deranged and scattered before the same enigma. Its luminous ray had not yet settled with sufficient rigidity and obstinacy on that dark point; and we should have once more said that Fatality is invincible. But, now, it held history and destiny in suspense for several weeks and ended by casting them without the brassbound track which they reckoned to follow to the end. Henceforth, if God, Chance, Justice, or whatever name we may give to the hidden idea of the universe, wish to attain their object, to go their way and triumph as before, they can follow other roads; but this one remains forbidden to them. In future, they will have to avoid the imperceptible but insuperable cleft where will always watch the little jet of flame that turned them back.

It is possible that this royal tragedy has definitely proved to us that wishes, love, pity, prayers, a whole portion of man's finest moral forces, are powerless in the face of one exercise of the will of nature. Immediately, as though to make good the loss and to maintain the rights of mind over matter at the necessary level, another moral force, or rather the same flame assuming another form, shoots up, shines forth and triumphs. Man loses an illusion to gain a certainty. Far from descending, he rises by one step among the unconscious forces. We have here, in spite of all the misery that surrounds it, a great and noble spectacle and something wherewith to arrest the attention of those who would lose confidence in the destinies of our kind.

UNIVERSAL SUFFRAGE

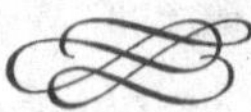

TRANSLATED BY ALEXANDER TEIXEIRA DE MATTOS.

I

It seems that gradually all is tending with one accord to prove that the last truths are at the extreme points of thoughts which man has hitherto refused to explore. This may be stated with regard to both moral and positive science; nor is there any reason against adding to these the science of politics, which is only a prolongation of moral science.

For centuries, mankind has, in a measure, lived in a half-way house. A thousand prejudices and, above all, the enormous prejudices of religion hid from it the summits of its reason and of its feelings. Now that the greater number of the artificial mountains that rose between its eyes and the real horizon of its mind have, in a marked manner, subsided, it takes stock at once of itself, of its position in the midst of the worlds and of the aim which it wishes to attain. It is beginning to understand that all that does not go as far as the logical conclusions of its intelligence is but a useless game by the way-side. It says to itself that it will have to cover to-morrow the road which it did not travel to-day and that, in the meantime, by thus wasting its time between every stage, it has nothing to gain but a little delusive peace.

It is written in our nature that we are extreme beings; that is our force and the cause of our progress. We necessarily and instinctively fly to the utmost limits of our being. We do not feel ourselves to live and we are unable to organize a life that shall satisfy us, except upon the confines of our possibilities. Thanks to that self-enlightening instinct, there is a more and more unanimous tendency to stop no longer at intermediate solutions, to avoid henceforth all half-way experiments or at least to hurry through them as rapidly as possible.

II

This does not mean that our tendency towards extremes is enough to guide us to definite certainties. There are always two extremes between which we have to choose; and it is often difficult to decide which is the starting-point and which the final goal. In morals, for instance, we have to choose between absolute egotism or altruism and in politics between the best-organized government that it is possible to imagine, directing and protecting the smallest acts of our life, or the absence of all government. The two questions are still insoluble. Nevertheless, we are free to believe that absolute altruism is more extreme and nearer to our end than absolute egotism, in the same way as anarchy is more extreme and nearer to the perfection of our kind than the most minutely and irreproachably organized government, such as, for instance, one might imagine to prevail at the last limits of integral socialism. We are free to believe this, because absolute altruism and anarchy are the extreme forms that demand the most perfect man. Now it is towards perfect man that we must turn our gaze; for it is in that direction that we must hope that mankind is moving. Experience still shows that we risk less by keeping our eyes before us than by keeping them behind us, less by looking too high than by not looking high enough. All that we have obtained so far has been announced and, so to speak, called forth by those who were accused of looking too high. It is wise, therefore, when in doubt, to attach one's self to the extreme that implies the most perfect, the most noble and the most generous form of mankind. Thus it was that this reply could be given to one who asked whether it were well to grant to men, in spite of their present imperfections, the most complete possible liberty:

"Yes, it is the duty of all whose thoughts go before the inconscient mass to destroy all that trammels the liberty of men, as if all men deserved to be free, even though we know that they will not deserve to be so until long after their deliverance. The harmonious use of liberty is acquired only by a long misuse of its benefits. By proceeding at the first to the most distant and highest ideal we have the greatest chance of afterwards discovering the best."

And what is true of liberty is also true of the other rights of man.

III

In order to apply this principle to universal suffrage, let us recall the political evolution of modern nations. It follows a uniform and inflexible curve. One by one, these nations escape from tyranny. A more or less aristocratic or plutocratic government, elected by a restricted suffrage, replaces the autocrat. This government, in its turn, makes way, or is almost everywhere on the point of making way for the government of all by universal suffrage. Where will the latter end? Will it bring us back to tyranny? Will it turn into a graduated suffrage? Will it become a sort of mandarinate, the government of a chosen few, or an organized anarchy? We can not yet tell, no nation having hitherto gone beyond the phase of the suffrage of all.

IV

Almost everywhere, in obedience to the now so active law that carries us to extremes, men are hurrying along at full speed the sooner to reach what appears to be the last political ideal of the nations, universal suffrage. Since this ideal still completely masks the better ideal that probably lies hidden behind it and since it does not appear what it perhaps is, a provisional solution, it will, until we have exhausted all the illusions which it contains, hold the gaze and wishes of humanity. It is the necessary goal, good or bad, towards which the nations are advancing. It is indispensable to the instinctive justice of the mass that the evolution should be accomplished. Anything that trammels it is but an ephemeral obstacle. Anything that pretends to improve that ideal before it has been attained drives it back towards the error of the past. Like every universal and imperious ideal, like every ideal formed in the depth of anonymous life, it has first of all the right to see itself realized. If, after its realization, it should become apparent that the ideal does not fulfil its promise, it will then be meet that we should think of perfecting or replacing it. In the meantime, this fact is inscribed in the instinct of the mass, as indestructibly as in bronze, that all nations have the natural right to pass through this phase of the political evolution of the human polypier and, each in its turn, each in its own language, with its particular virtues and faults, to interrogate the possibilities of happiness which it brings.

That is why, full of the duty of living, this ideal is most justly jealous, intolerant and unreasonable. Like every youthful organism, it violently eliminates all that can impair the purity of its blood. It is possible that the elements borrowed from monarchy and aristocracy which men endeavour to introduce into its adolescent veins are excellent in themselves; but they are injurious to it because they inoculate it with the ill of which it has first to be cured. Before the government of all can be made wiser, more limpid and more harmonious by the admixture of other systems, it must have purified itself by its own fermentation. After it has rid itself of every trace, of every memory of the past, after it has reigned in the certainty and integrity of its force, then will be the time to invite it to choose in the past that which concerns its future. It will take of this according to its natural appetite, which, like the natural appetite of every living being, knows with a sure knowledge what is indispensable to the mystery of life.

V

The nations are right therefore in provisionally rejecting that which is, perhaps, better than universal suffrage. It is possible that the crowd will eventually admit that the more highly intelligent discern and govern the common weal better than the others. It will then grant them a lawful preponderance. For the moment, it does not give them a thought. It has not had time to learn to know itself. It has not had time to exhaust experiments which appear absurd, but which are necessary because they clear the place in which the last truths without doubt lie hidden.

It is with nations as with individuals: that which tells is what they learn by themselves, at their own cost; and their mistakes form the heritage of the future. It serves no purpose to say to a man in his childhood or in his youth:

"Do not lie, do not deceive, cause no suffering."

Those precepts of wisdom, which are at the same time precepts of happiness, do not impress him, do not feed his thoughts, do not become beneficent realities until after the moment when life has revealed them to him as new and magnificent truths which no one ever suspected. In the same way, it is useless to repeat to a nation that is seeking out its destiny:

"Do not believe that the multitude is right, that a lie stated by a hundred mouths ceases to be a lie, that an error proclaimed by a band of blind men becomes a truth which nature will sanction. Do not believe, either, that, by setting yourselves to the number of ten thousand who do not know against one who knows, you will come to know anything, or that you will compel the humblest of the eternal laws to follow you, to abandon him who recognized it. No, the law will remain in its place, with the wise man who discovered it, and so much the worse for you if you go away without accepting it! You will one day come across it on your road, and all that you have done while you thought that you were avoiding it will turn and rise up against you."

Such words as these, addressed to the crowd, are very true; but it is no less true that all this becomes efficacious only after it has been experienced and lived through. In those problems in which all life's enigmas converge, the crowd which is wrong is almost always justified as against the wise man who is right. It refuses to believe him on his word. It feels dimly that behind the most evident abstract truths there are numberless living truths which no brain can foresee, for they need time, reality and men's passions to develop their work. That is why, whatever warning we may give it, whatever prediction we may make to it, the crowd insists before all that the experiment shall be tried. Can we say that, in cases where the crowd has obtained the experiment, it was wrong to insist upon it?

A special study would be needed to examine all that universal suffrage has added to the general intelligence, to the civic conscience, dignity and solidarity of the nations that have practised it; but, even if it had done no more than to create, as in America and France, that sense of real equality which is there breathed as a more human and purer atmosphere and which seems new and almost prodigious to those who come from elsewhere, that in itself would be a boon that would cause its gravest errors to be forgiven. In any case, it is the best preparation for that which must inevitably come.

THE MODERN DRAMA

TRANSLATED BY ALFRED SUTRO.

I

When I speak of the modern drama, I naturally refer only to those regions of dramatic literature that, sparsely inhabited as they may be, are yet essentially new. Down below, in the ordinary theatre, ordinary and traditional drama is doubtless yielding slowly to the influence of the vanguard; but it were idle to wait for the laggards when we have the pioneers at our call.

The first thing that strikes us in the drama of the day is the decay, one might almost say the creeping paralysis, of external action. Next we note a very pronounced desire to penetrate deeper and deeper into human consciousness, and place moral problems upon a high pedestal; and finally the search, still very timid and halting, for a kind of new beauty, that shall be less abstract than was the old.

It is certain that, on the actual stage, we have far fewer

extraordinary and violent adventures. Bloodshed has grown less frequent, passions less turbulent; heroism has become less unbending, courage less material and less ferocious. People still die on the stage, it is true, as in reality they still must die, but death has ceased —or will cease, let us hope, very soon—to be regarded as the indispensable setting, the *ultima ratio*, the inevitable end, of every dramatic poem. In the most formidable crises of our life—which, cruel though it may be, is cruel in silent and hidden ways—we rarely look to death for a solution; and for all that the theatre is slower than the other arts to follow the evolution of human consciousness, it will still be at last compelled, in some measure, to take this into account.

When we consider the ancient and tragical anecdotes that constitute the entire basis of the classical drama; the Italian, Scandinavian, Spanish or mythical stories that provided the plots, not only for all the plays of the Shakespearian period, but also—not altogether to pass over an art that was infinitely less spontaneous—for those of French and German romanticism, we discover at once that these anecdotes are no longer able to offer us the direct interest they presented at a time when they appeared highly natural and possible, at a time, when, at any rate, the circumstances, manners and sentiments they recalled were not yet extinct in the minds of those who witnessed their reproduction.

II

To us, however, these adventures no longer correspond with a living and actual reality. Should a youth of our own time love, and meet obstacles not unlike those which, in another order of ideas and events, beset Romeo's passion, we need no telling that his adventure will be embellished by none of the features that gave poetry and grandeur to the episode of Verona. Gone beyond recall is the entrancing atmosphere of a lordly, passionate life; gone the brawls in picturesque streets, the interludes of bloodshed and splendour, the mysterious poisons, the majestic, complaisant tombs! And where shall we look for that exquisite summer's night, which owes its vastness, its savour, the very appeal that it makes to us, to the shadow of an heroic, inevitable death that already lay heavy upon it? Divest the story of Romeo and Juliet of these beautiful trappings, and we have only the very simple and ordinary desire of a noble-hearted, unfortunate youth for a maiden whose obdurate parents deny him her hand. All the poetry, the splendour, the passionate life of this desire, result from the glamour, the nobility, tragedy, that are proper to the environment wherein it has come to flower; nor is there a kiss, a murmur of love, a cry of anger, grief or despair, but borrows its majesty, grace, its heroism, tenderness—in a word, every image that has helped it to visible form—from the beings and objects around it; for it is not in the kiss itself that the sweetness and beauty are found, but in the circumstance, hour and place wherein it was given. Again, the same objections would hold if we chose to imagine a man of our time who should be jealous as Othello was jealous, possessed of Macbeth's ambition, unhappy as Lear; or, like Hamlet, restless and wavering, bowed down beneath the weight of a frightful and unrealisable duty.

III

These conditions no longer exist. The adventure of the modern Romeo—to consider only the external events which it might provoke—would not provide material for a couple of acts. Against this it may be urged that a modern poet, who desires to put on the stage an analogous poem of youthful love, is perfectly justified in borrowing from days gone by a more decorative setting, one that shall be more fertile in heroic and tragical incident. Granted; but what can the result be of such an expedient? Would not the feelings and passions that demand for their fullest, most perfect expression and development the atmosphere of to-day (for the passions and feelings of a modern poet must, in despite of himself, be entirely and exclusively modern) would not these suddenly find themselves transplanted to a soil where all things prevented their living? They no longer believe, yet are charged with the fear and hope of eternal judgment. In their hours of distress they have discovered new forces to cling to, that seem trustworthy, human and just; and behold them thrust back to a century wherein prayer and the sword decide all! They have profited, unconsciously perhaps, by every moral advance we have made—and they are suddenly flung into abysmal days when the least gesture was governed by prejudices at which they can only shudder or smile. In such an atmosphere, what can they do; how hope that they truly can live there?

IV

But we need dwell no further on the necessarily artificial poems that arise from the impossible marriage of past and present. Let us rather consider the drama that actually stands for the reality of our time, as Greek drama stood for Greek reality, and the drama of the Renaissance for the reality of the Renaissance. Its scene is a modern house, it passes between men and women of to-day. The names of the invisible protagonists—the passions and ideas—are the same, more or less, as of old. We see love, hatred, ambition, jealousy, envy, greed; the sense of justice and idea of duty; pity, goodness, devotion, piety, selfishness, vanity, pride, etc. But although the names have remained more or less the same, how great is the difference we find in the aspect and quality, the extent and influence, of these ideal actors! Of all their ancient weapons not one is left them, not one of the marvellous moments of olden days. It is seldom that cries are heard now; bloodshed is rare, and tears not often seen. It is in a small room, round a table, close to the fire, that the joys and sorrows of mankind are decided. We suffer, or make others suffer, we love, we die, there in our corner; and it were the strangest chance should a door or a window suddenly, for an instant, fly open, beneath the pressure of extraordinary despair or rejoicing. Accidental, adventitious beauty exists no longer; there remains only an external poetry, that has not yet become poetic.—And what poetry, if we probe to the root of things—what poetry is there that does not borrow nearly all of its charm, nearly all of its ecstasy, from elements that are wholly external?—Last of all, there is no longer a God to widen, or master, the action; nor is there an inexorable fate to form a mysterious, solemn and tragical background for the slightest gesture of man; nor the sombre and abundant atmosphere, that was able to ennoble even his most contemptible weaknesses, his least pardonable crimes.

There still abides with us, it is true, a terrible unknown; but it is so diverse and elusive, it becomes so arbitrary, so vague and contradictory, the moment we try to locate it, that we cannot evoke it without great danger; cannot even, without the mightiest difficulty, avail ourselves of it, though in all loyalty, to raise to the point of mystery the gestures, actions and words of the men we pass every day. The endeavour has been made; the formidable, problematic enigma of heredity, the grandiose but improbable enigma of inherent justice, and many others besides, have each in their turn been put forward as a substitute for the vast enigma of the Providence or Fatality of old. And it is curious to note how these youthful enigmas, born but of yesterday, already seem older, more arbitrary, more unlikely, than those whose places they took in an access of pride.

V

Where are we to look, then, for the grandeur and beauty that we find no longer in visible action, or in words, stripped as these are of their attraction and glamour? For words are only a kind of mirror which reflects the beauty of all that surrounds it; and the beauty of the new world wherein we live does not seem as yet able to project its rays on these somewhat reluctant mirrors. Where shall we look for the horizon, the poetry, now that we no longer can seek it in a mystery which, for all that it still exists, does yet fade from us the moment we endeavour to give it a name?

The modern drama would seem to be vaguely conscious of this. Incapable of outside movement, deprived of external ornament, daring no longer to make serious appeal to a determined divinity or fatality, it has fallen back on itself, and seeks to discover, in the regions of psychology and of moral problems, the equivalent of what once was offered by exterior life. It has penetrated deeper into human consciousness; but has encountered difficulties there no less strange than unexpected.

To penetrate deeply into human consciousness is the privilege, even the duty, of the thinker, the moralist, the historian, novelist, and to a degree, of the lyrical poet; but not of the dramatist. Whatever the temptation, he dare not sink into inactivity, become mere philosopher or observer. Do what one will, discover what marvels one may, the sovereign law of the stage, its essential demand, will always be *action*. With the rise of the curtain, the high intellectual desire within us undergoes transformation; and in place of the thinker, psychologist, mystic or moralist there stands the mere instinctive spectator, the man electrified negatively by the crowd, the man whose one desire it is to see something happen. This transformation or substitution is incontestable, strange as it may seem; and is due, perhaps, to the influence of the *human polypier*, to some undeniable faculty of our soul, which is endowed with a special, primitive, almost unimprovable organ, whereby men can think, and feel, and be moved, *en masse*. And there are no words so profound, so noble and admirable, but they will soon weary us if they leave the situation unchanged, if they lead to no action, bring about no decisive conflict, or hasten no definite solution.

VI

But whence is it that action arises in the consciousness of man? In its first stage it springs from the struggle between diverse conflicting passions. But no sooner has it raised itself somewhat— and this is true, if we examine it closely, of the first stage also— than it would seem to be solely due to the conflict between a passion and a moral law, between a duty and a desire. Hence the eagerness with which modern dramatists have plunged into all the problems of contemporary morality; and it may safely be said that at this moment they confine themselves almost exclusively to the discussion of these different problems.

This movement was initiated by the dramas of Alexandre Dumas fils, dramas which brought the most elementary of moral conflicts on to the stage; dramas, indeed, whose entire existence was based on problems such as the spectator, who must always be regarded as the ideal moralist, would never put to himself in the course of his whole spiritual existence, so evident is their solution. Should the faithless husband or wife be forgiven? Is it well to avenge infidelity by infidelity? Has the illegitimate child any rights? Is the marriage of inclination—such is the name it bears in those regions—preferable to the marriage for money? Have parents the right to oppose a marriage for love? Is divorce to be deprecated when a child has been born of the union? Is the sin of the adulterous wife greater than that of the adulterous husband? etc., etc.

Indeed, it may be said here that the entire French theatre of to-day, and a considerable proportion of the foreign theatre, which is only its echo, exist solely on questions of this kind, and on the entirely superfluous answers to which they give rise.

On the other hand, however, the highest point of human consciousness is attained by the dramas of Björnson, of Hauptmann, and, above all, of Ibsen. Here we touch the limit of the resources of modern dramaturgy. For, in truth, the further we penetrate into the consciousness of man, the less struggle do we discover. It is impossible to penetrate far into any consciousness unless that consciousness be very enlightened; for, whether we advance ten steps, or a thousand, in the depths of a soul that is plunged in darkness, we shall find nothing there that can be unexpected, or new; for darkness everywhere will only resemble itself. But a consciousness that is truly enlightened will possess passions and desires infinitely less exacting, infinitely more peaceful and patient, more salutary, abstract and general, than are those that reside in the ordinary consciousness. Thence, far less struggle—or at least a struggle of far less violence—between these nobler and wiser passions; and this for the very reason that they have become vaster and loftier; for if there be nothing more restless, destructive and savage than a dammed-up stream, there is nothing more tranquil, beneficent and silent than the beautiful river whose banks ever widen.

VII

Again, this enlightened consciousness will yield to infinitely fewer laws, admit infinitely fewer doubtful or harmful duties. There is, one may say, scarcely a falsehood or error, a prejudice, half-truth or convention, that is not capable of assuming, that does not actually assume, when the occasion presents itself, the form of a duty in an uncertain consciousness. It is thus that honour, in the chivalrous, conjugal sense of the word (I refer to the honour of the husband, which is supposed to suffer by the infidelity of the wife) that revenge, a kind of morbid prudishness, pride, vanity, piety to certain gods, and a thousand other illusions, have been, and still remain, the unquenchable source of a multitude of duties that are still regarded as absolutely sacred, absolutely incontrovertible, by a vast number of inferior consciousnesses. And these so-called duties are the pivot of almost all the dramas of the Romantic period, as of most of those of to-day. But not one of these sombre, pitiless duties, that so fatally impel mankind to death and disaster, can readily take root in the consciousness that a healthy, living light has adequately penetrated; in such there will be no room for honour or vengeance, for conventions that clamour for blood. It will hold no prejudices that exact tears, no injustice eager for sorrow. It will have cast from their throne the gods who insist on sacrifice, and the love that craves for death. For when the sun has entered into the consciousness of him who is wise, as we may hope that it will some day enter into that of all men, it will reveal one duty, and one alone, which is that we should do the least possible harm and love others as we love ourselves; and from this duty no drama can spring.

VIII

Let us consider what happens in Ibsen's plays. He often leads us far down into human consciousness, but the drama remains possible only because there goes with us a singular flame, a sort of red light, which, sombre, capricious—unhallowed, one almost might say— falls only on singular phantoms. And indeed nearly all the duties which form the active principle of Ibsen's tragedies are duties situated no longer within, but without, the healthy, illumined consciousness; and the duties we believe we discover outside this consciousness often come perilously near an unjust pride, or a kind of soured and morbid madness.

Let it not be imagined, however—for indeed this would be wholly to misunderstand me—that these remarks of mine in any way detract from my admiration for the great Scandinavian poet. For, if it be true that Ibsen has contributed few salutary elements to the morality of our time, he is perhaps the only writer for the stage who has caught sight of, and set in motion, a new, though still disagreeable poetry, which he has succeeded in investing with a kind of age, gloomy beauty and grandeur (surely too savage and gloomy for it to become general or definitive); as he is the only one who owes nothing to the poetry of the violently illumined dramas of antiquity or of the Renaissance.

But, while we wait for the time when human consciousness shall recognise more useful passions and less nefarious duties, for the time when the world's stage shall consequently present more happiness and fewer tragedies, there still remains, in the depths of every heart of loyal intention a great duty of charity and justice that eclipses all others. And it is perhaps from the struggle of this duty against our egoism and ignorance that the veritable drama of our century shall spring. When this goal has been attained—in real life as on the stage—it will be permissible perhaps to speak of a new theatre, a theatre of peace, and of beauty without tears.

THE FORETELLING OF THE FUTURE

TRANSLATED BY ALEXANDER TEIXEIRA DE MATTOS.

I

It is, in certain respects, quite inexplicable that we should not know the Future. Probably a mere nothing, the displacement of a cerebral lobe, the resetting of Broca's convolution in a different manner, the addition of a slender network of nerves to those which form our consciousness: any one of these would be enough to make the future unfold itself before us with the same clearness, the same majestic amplitude as that with which the past is displayed on the horizon not only of our individual life, but also of the life of the species to which we belong. A singular infirmity, a curious limitation of our intellect causes us not to know what is going to happen to us, when we are fully aware of all that has befallen us. From the absolute point of view to which our imagination succeeds in rising, although it cannot live there, there is no reason why we should not see that which does not yet exist, considering that that which does not yet exist in its relation to us must needs already have its being and manifest itself somewhere. If not, it would have to be said that, where Time is concerned, we form the centre of the world, that we are the only witnesses for whom events wait so that they may have the right to appear and to count in the eternal history of causes and effects. It would be as absurd to assert this for Time as it would be for Space, that other not quite so incomprehensible form of the two-fold infinite mystery in which our whole life floats.

Space is more familiar to us, because the accidents of our organism place us more directly in relation with it and make it more concrete. We can move in it pretty freely, in a certain number of directions before and behind us. That is why no traveller would take it into his head to maintain that the towns which he has not yet visited will become real only at the moment when he sets his foot within their walls. Yet this is very nearly what we do when we persuade ourselves that an event which has not yet happened does not yet exist.

II

But I do not intend, in the wake of so many others, to lose myself in the most insoluble of enigmas. Let us say no more about it, except this alone, that Time is a mystery which we have arbitrarily divided into a Past and a Future, in order to try to understand something of it. In itself we may be almost certain that it is but an immense eternal, motionless Present, in which all that takes place and all that will take place takes place immutably, in which To-Morrow, save in the ephemeral mind of man, is indistinguishable from Yesterday or To-Day.

One would say that man had always the feeling that a mere infirmity of his mind separates him from the Future. He knows it to be there, living, actual, perfect, behind a kind of wall around which he has never ceased to turn since the first days of his coming on this earth. Or rather, he feels it within himself and known to a part of himself: only, that importunate and disquieting knowledge is unable to travel, through the too narrow channels of his senses, to his consciousness, which is the only place where knowledge acquires a name, a useful strength and, so to speak, the freedom of the human city. It is only by glimmers, by casual and passing infiltrations that future years of which he is full, of which the imperious realities surround him on every hand, penetrate to his brain. He marvels that an extraordinary accident should have closed almost hermetically to the Future that brain which plunges into it entirely, even as a sealed vessel plunges, without mixing with it, into the depths of a monstrous sea that overwhelms it, entreats it, teases it and caresses it with a thousand billows.

At all times, man has tried to find crannies in that wall, to provoke infiltrations into that vessel, to pierce the partitions that separate his reason, which knows scarcely anything, from his instinct, which knows all, but cannot make use of its knowledge. It seems as though he must have succeeded more than once. There have been visionaries, prophets, sibyls, pythonesses, in whom a distemper, a spontaneously or artificially hypertrophied nervous system permitted unwonted communications to be established between consciousness and unconsciousness, between the life of the individual and that of the species, between man and his hidden god. They have left evidences of this capacity which are as irrefutable as any other historical evidence. On the other hand, as those strange interpreters, those great mysterious hysterics, along whose nerves thus circulated and mingled the Present and the Past, were rare, men discovered, or thought that they discovered, empirical processes to enable them almost mechanically to read the ever-present and irritating riddle of the Future. They flattered themselves that, in this manner, they could consult the unconscious knowledge of things and beasts. Thence came the interpretation of the flight of birds, of the entrails of victims, of the course of the stars, of fire, water, dreams and all the methods of divination that have been handed down to us by the authors of antiquity.

III

I thought it curious to inquire where this science of the Future stands to-day. It no longer has the splendour nor the hardihood of old. It no longer forms part of the public and religious life of nations. The Present and the Past reveal so many prodigies to us that these suffice to amuse our thirst for marvels. Absorbed as we are in what is or was, we have almost given up asking what might be or will be. However, the old and venerable science, so deeply rooted in man's infallible instinct, is not abandoned. It is no longer practised in broad daylight. It has taken shelter in the darkest corners, in the most vulgar, credulous, ignorant and despised environments. It employs innocent or childish methods; nevertheless, it, too, has in a certain measure evolved, like other things. It neglects the majority of the processes of primitive divination; it has found others, often eccentric, sometimes ludicrous, and has been able to profit by some few discoveries that were by no means intended for it.

I have followed it into its dark retreats. I wished to see it, not in books, but at work, in real life, and among the humble faithful who have confidence in it and who daily apply to it for advice and encouragement. I went to it in good faith: unbelieving, but ready to believe; without prejudice and without a predetermined smile: for, if we must admit no miracle blindly, it is worse blindly to laugh at it; and in every obstinate error there lurks, usually, an excellent truth that awaits the hour of birth.

IV

Few towns would have offered me a wider or more fruitful field of experiment than Paris. I therefore made my investigations there. I began by selecting a moment at which a certain project, whose realization (which did not depend upon myself alone) was to be of great importance to me, was hanging in suspense. I will not enter into the details of the business, which has very little interest in itself. It is enough to know that around this project were a crowd of intrigues and many powerful and hostile wills, fighting against my own. The forces were evenly balanced, and it was impossible, according to human logic, to foresee which would win the day. I therefore had very precise questions to put to the Future: a necessary condition; for, if many people complain that it tells them nothing, this is often because they consult it at a moment when nothing is preparing on the horizon of their existence.

I went successively to see the astrologers, the palmists, the fallen and familiar sibyls who flatter themselves that they can read the Future in the cards, in coffee-grounds, in the inflorescence of white of egg dissolved in a glass of water, and so on (for nothing must be neglected, and, though the apparatus be sometimes singular, it may happen that a particle of truth lies concealed under the absurdest practices). I went, above all, to see the most famous of the prophetesses who, under the names of clairvoyants, seers, mediums, and the rest, are able to substitute for their own consciousness the consciousness and even a portion of the unconsciousness of their interrogators and who are, in the main, the most direct heiresses of the pythonesses of old. In this ill-balanced world, I met with much knavery, simulation and gross lying. But I had also the occasion to study certain incontestable phenomena close at hand. These are not enough to decide whether it be given to man to rend the tissue of illusions that hides the Future from him; but they throw a somewhat strange light upon that which passes in the place which to us seems the most inviolable, I mean the holy of holies of the "Buried Temple," in which our most intimate thoughts and the forces that lie beneath them and are unknown to us go in and out without our knowledge and grope in search of the mysterious road that leads to future events.

V

It would be wearisome to relate what happened to me with those prophets and seers. I will content myself with briefly telling one of the most curious experiences, which, moreover, sums up most of the others: the psychology of them all is very nearly identical.

The seer in question is one of the most famous in Paris. She claims to incarnate, in her hypnotic state, the spirit of an unknown little girl called Julia. Having made me sit down at a table that stood between us, she begged me to *tutoyer* Julia and to speak to her gently, as one speaks to a child of seven or eight years. Thereupon, her features, her eyes, her hands, her whole body were for some seconds unpleasantly convulsed; her hair came untied; and the expression of her face changed completely and became artless, puerile. The voice, shrill and clear, of a small child next came from that great, ripe woman's body and asked with a little lisp:

"What do you want? Are you troubled? Is it for yourself or for some one else that you have come to see me?"

"For myself."

"Very well; will you help me a little? Lead me in thought to the place where your troubles are."

I concentrated my attention on the project in which I was engrossed and on the different actors in the, as yet, hidden little drama. Then, gradually, after some preliminary gropings, and without my helping her with a word or gesture, she really penetrated into my thoughts, read them, so to speak, as a slightly veiled book, placed the situation of the scene most accurately, recognized the principal characters and described them summarily, with hopping and childish, but quaintly correct and precise little touches.

"That's very good, Julia," I then said, "but I know all that; what you ought to tell me is what is going to happen later."

"What is going to happen, what is going to happen ... you want to know all that is going to happen, but it's very difficult...."

"But still? How will the business end? Shall I win?"

"Yes, yes, I see; don't be afraid, I'll help you; you will be pleased...."

"But the enemy of whom you told me; the one who is resisting me and who wishes me ill...."

"No, no, he wishes you no ill, it's because of some one else.... I can't see why.... He hates him.... Oh, he hates him, he hates him! And it is because you like the other one so much that he does not want you to do for him what you wish to do."

What she said was true.

"But tell me," I insisted, "will he go on to the end, will he not yield?"

"Oh, do not fear him.... I see, he is ill; he will not live long."

"You are mistaken, Julia; I saw him two days ago; he is quite well."

"No, no, he is ill.... It doesn't show, but he is very ill ... he must die soon...."

"But how, in that case, and why?"

"There is blood upon him, around him, everywhere...."

"Blood? Is it a duel?" (I had thought, for a moment, that I might be called upon to fight my adversary.) "An accident, a murder, a revenge?" (He was an unjust and unscrupulous man, who had done much harm to many people.)

"No, no, ask me no more, I am very tired.... Let me go...."

"Not before I know...."

"No, I can tell you nothing more.... I am too tired.... Let me go.... Be good, I will help you...."

The same attack as at first then convulsed the body, in which the little voice had ceased; and the mask of forty years again covered the face of the woman, who seemed to be waking from a long sleep.

Is it necessary to add that we had never seen each other before this meeting and that we knew as little of each other as though we had been born on different planets?

VI

Similar in the main, with less characteristic and less convincing details, were the results of most of the experiments in which the clairvoyants were unfeignedly asleep. In order to make a sort of counter-test, I sent two persons of whose intelligence and good faith I was assured, to see the woman whom Julia had chosen as her interpreter. Like myself, they had to put to the Future a precise and important question, which chance or destiny alone could solve. To one of them, who consulted her on a friend's illness, Julia foretold the near death of that friend, and the event verified her prediction, although, at the moment when she made it, a cure seemed infinitely more probable than death. To the other, who asked her how a lawsuit would end, she replied somewhat evasively on that point; by way of compensation she spontaneously revealed the spot where lay a certain object which had been very precious to the person consulting her, but which had been so long lost and so often looked for in vain that this person was persuaded that he had ceased to think about it.

In so far as I am concerned, Julia's prophecy was realized in part, that is to say, although I did not triumph in respect of the main point, the affair was nevertheless arranged in a satisfactory manner.

As for the death of my adversary, it has not yet occurred; and gladly do I dispense the Future from keeping the promise which it made me by the innocent mouth of the child of an unknown world.

VII

It is very astonishing that others can thus penetrate into the last refuge of our being and there, better than ourselves, read thoughts and sentiments at times forgotten or rejected, but always long-lived, or as yet unformulated. It is really disconcerting that a stranger should see further than ourselves into our own hearts. That sheds a singular light on the nature of our inner lives. It is vain for us to keep watch upon ourselves, to shut ourselves up within ourselves: our consciousness is not watertight, it escapes, it does not belong to us; and, though it requires special circumstances for another to instal himself there and take possession of it, nevertheless it is certain that, in normal life, our spiritual tribunal, our *for intérieur*—as the French have called it, with that profound intuition which we often discover in the etymology of words—is a kind of *forum*, or spiritual market-place, in which the majority of those who have business there come and go at will, look about them and pick out the truths, in a very different fashion and much more freely than we would have believed.

But let us leave this point, which is not the object of our study. What I should like to unravel in Julia's predictions is the unknown part foreign to myself. Did she go beyond what I knew? I do not think so. When she spoke to me of the fortunate issue of the affair, this was, upon the whole, the issue which I anticipated and which the selfish and unavowed part of my instinct desired more keenly than the complete triumph which another and more generous senti-ment made it incumbent on me to pursue and hope for, although I knew it to be, in its essence, impossible. When she foretold the death of my adversary, she was but revealing a secret wish of that same instinct, one of those dastardly and shameful wishes which we hide from ourselves and which never rise to the surface of our thought. There would be no real prophecy in this, except if, against all expectation, against all likelihood, that death should occur, suddenly, within a short time hence. But, even if it were shortly to occur, it would not, I think, be the Pythian that would have fathomed the Future, but I, my instinct, my unconscious being, that would have foreseen an event with which it was connected. It would have read the pages of Time, not absolutely and as though in an universal book where all that is to take place is written, but by me, through me, in my private intuition, and would but have translated what my unconsciousness was unable to communicate to my thought.

It was the same, I imagine, with the two persons who went to consult her. That one to whom she foretold the death of a friend probably, in spite of the assurance which reason gave to friendship, had the inner conviction, either natural or conjectural, but violently suppressed, that the sick man would die; and it was this conviction which the clairvoyant discerned amid the sweet hopes that strove to deceive it. As for the second, who unexpectedly recovered a mislaid object, it is difficult to know the state of another's mind with sufficient exactness to decide whether this was a case of second sight, or simply of recollection. Was he who had lost the object absolutely ignorant of the place and circumstances in which he had lost it? He says so; he declares that he never had the least notion: that, on the contrary, he was persuaded that the object had been not mislaid, but stolen, and that he had never ceased to suspect one of his servants. But it is possible that, while his intelligence, his waking *ego*, paid no attention to it, the unconscious and as though sleeping portion of himself may very well have remarked and remembered the place where the object had been put. Thence, by a miracle no less surprising, but of a different order, the seer would have found and awakened the latent and almost animal memory and brought it to human light which it had vainly tried to reach.

VIII

Could this be the case with all predictions? Were the prophecies of the great prophets, the oracles of the sibyls, witches, pythonesses content thus to reflect, translate, raise to the level of the intelligible world the instinctive clairvoyance of the individuals or peoples that listened to them? Let each accept the reply or the hypothesis which his own experience suggests to him. I have given mine with the simplicity and sincerity which a question of this nature demands.*

------

* Other subjects of my inquiries gave me less curious, but often analogous results. I visited, for instance, a certain number of palmists. On seeing the sumptuous apartments of several of those prophets of the hand, who revealed to me nothing but nonsense, I was admiring the ingenuousness of their patrons, when a friend pointed out to me, in a lane near the Mont-de-Piété, the abode of a practitioner who, according to him, had most effectively cultivated and developed the great traditions of the science of Desbarolles and d'Arpentigny.

On the sixth floor of a hideous rabbit-warren of a house, in a loft that served as both living-room and bed-room, I found an unpretending, gentle and vulgar old man, whose manner of speech suggested the hall-porter rather than the prophet. I did not obtain much from him; but, in the case of some more nervous persons whom I brought to him, particularly two or three women with whose past and character I was fairly well-acquainted, he revealed with rather astonishing precision the essential preoccupations of their minds and hearts, discerned very cleverly the chief curves of their existence, stopped at the cross-roads where their destinies had really swerved or wavered, and discovered certain strikingly exact and almost anecdotical particulars, such as journeys, love-affairs, influences undergone, or accidents. In a word, and taking into consideration the sort of auto-suggestion that causes our imagination, more or less inflamed by the contact of mystery, immediately and precisely to state the most shapeless clue, he traced, on a somewhat conventional and symbolical plan, a clearly-established scheme of their past and present, in which they were obliged, in spite of their distrust, to recognize the special track of their lives. In so far as his predictions are concerned, I must say, in passing, that not one of them was realized.

To resume my inquiry. In so far, then, as concerns that formidable unknown which stretches before us, I found nothing conclusive, nothing decisive; and yet, I repeat, it is almost incredible that we should not know the Future. I can imagine that we stand opposite to it as though opposite to a forgotten past. We might try to remember it. It would be a question of inventing or re-discovering the road taken by that memory which precedes us.

I can conceive that we are not qualified to know beforehand the disturbances of the elements, the destiny of the planets of the earth, of empires, peoples and races. All this does not touch us directly, and we know it in the past thanks only to the artifices of history. But that which regards us, that which is within our reach, that which is to unfold itself within the little sphere of years, a secretion of our spiritual organism, that envelops us in Time, even as the shell or the cocoon envelops the mollusc or the insect in Space; that, together with all the external events relating to it, is probably recorded in that sphere. In any case, it would be much more natural that it were so recorded than comprehensible that it were not. There we have realities struggling with an illusion; and there is nothing to prevent us from believing that, here as elsewhere, realities will end by overcoming illusion. Realities are what will happen to us, having already happened in the history that overhangs our own, the motionless and superhuman history of the universe. Illusion is the opaque veil woven with the ephemeral threads called Yesterday, To-day and To-Morrow, which we embroider on those realities. But it is not

---

Certainly there was in his intuition something more than a fortunate coincidence. It was, in a lesser degree, a sort of nervous communication between one unconsciousness and another of the same class, as with the clairvoyant. I have met the same phenomenon in the case of a woman who read coffee-grounds, but accompanied by more venturesome and less certain manifestations: I will, therefore, not pause to consider it.

indispensable that our existence should continue the eternal dupe of that illusion. We may even ask ourselves whether our extraordinary unfitness for knowing a thing so simple, so incontestable, so perfect and so unnecessary as the Future, would not form one of the greatest subjects for astonishment to an inhabitant of another star who should visit us.

To-day, all this appears to us so profoundly impossible that we find it difficult to imagine how the certain reality of the Future would refute the objections which we make to it in the name of the organic illusion of our minds. We say to it, for instance: If, at the moment of undertaking an affair, we could know that its outcome would be unfortunate, we should not undertake it; and, since it must be written somewhere, in Time, before our question has been put, that the affair will not take place, seeing that we abandon it, we could not, therefore, foresee the outcome of that which will have no beginning.

So as not to lose ourselves in this road, which would lead us whither nothing calls us, it will be enough for us to say that the Future, like all that exists, is probably more coherent and more logical than the logic of our imagination and that all our hesitations and uncertainties are included in its provisions.

Moreover, we must not believe that the march of events would be completely upset if we knew it beforehand. First, only they would know the Future, or a part of the Future, who would take the trouble to learn it; even as only they know the Past, or a part of their own Present, who have the courage and the intelligence to examine it. We should quickly accommodate ourselves to the lessons of this new science, even as we have accommodated ourselves to those of history. We should soon make allowance for the evils which we could not escape and for inevitable evils. The wiser among us, for themselves, would lessen the sum total of the latter; and the others would meet them half-way, even as now they go to meet many certain disasters which are easily foretold. The amount of our vexations would be somewhat decreased, but less than we hope; for already our reason is able to foresee a portion of our Future, if not with the material evidence that we dream of, at least with a moral certainty that is often satisfying: yet we observe that the majority of men derive hardly any profit from this easy foreknowledge. Such men would neglect the counsels of the Future, even as they hear, without following it, the advice of the Past.

IN AN AUTOMOBILE

TRANSLATED BY ALFRED SUTRO.

I

The first trips—the initiation, with the master's eye upon you—count for but little. One is not in direct communication with the wonderful beast. Its veritable character is hidden, for there is a tiresome intermediary between, a reticent, cunning interpreter—the responsible tamer. With your foot on the brake, even when you hold the levers and handles between your fingers, you are far from possessing the monster. By your side sits the master, whose sovereignty it has too long acknowledged; to him it is as obsequious, as submissively attached, as a faithful dog. For the thing is half human. You feel somewhat like a lion-tamer's apprentice when he enters the cage with his father, and sees the cowed brutes prostrate themselves humbly before the commanding eye and the lash. One has a great desire to be alone, in Space, with this unknown animal, that dates but from yesterday; we burn to discover what it is in itself, what it demands and withholds, what obedience it will vouchsafe to its unexpected master; as also what new lessons the new horizons will teach us, the new horizons into which we shall be plunged to our very soul by a force that, issuing now, and for the first time, from the inexhaustible reservoir of undisciplined forces, permits us to absorb, in one day, as many sights, as much landscape and sky, as would formerly have been granted to us in a whole lifetime.

II

Yesterday the master drove us from Paris to Rouen. This morning he left me, having first taken me outside the gates of the old, many-steepled city. There I was, alone with the dreadful hippogriff; alone in the open country, the horizon of immaculate blue on the left, on the right still faintly pink; alone on the desolate road that winds between oceans of corn, with islands of trees that turn into blue in the distance.

I am many miles from a station, far from garage or repairers. And at first I am conscious of a vague uneasiness, that is not without its charm. I am at the mercy of this mysterious force, that is yet more logical than I. A caprice of its hidden life—one of those caprices that, mysterious as they may seem to us, are yet never wrong, and put our arrogant reason to shame—and I should be solitary in this illimitable vastness of green, chained to the enigmatic mass that my arms cannot move. But the monster, I say to myself, has no secrets that I have not learned. Before placing myself in its power, I took it to pieces, and examined its organs. And, now that it snorts at my feet, I can recall its physiology. I know its infallible wheelwork, its delicate points; I have studied its infantile maladies, and learned what diseases are fatal. I have had its heart and soul laid bare, I have looked into the profound circulation of its life. Its soul is the electric spark, which, seven or eight hundred times to the minute, sends fiery breath through the veins. And the terrible, complex heart is composed, first of all, of the carburetter, with its strange double face: the carburetter, which prepares, proportions and volatilizes the petrol—subtle fairy that has slumbered ever since the world began, and is now recalled to power, and united to the air that has torn her from sleep. This redoubtable mixture is eagerly swallowed by the mighty viscera close by, which contain the explosion chamber, the piston, all the live force of the motor. And around these, which form one mass of flame, pure water circulates always, restraining the passionate ardour that else would devour them and turn them into a flow of lava, calming with its long and icy caress the mortal frenzy of toil—vigilant, untiring water, that the radiator posted in front of the car keeps cool, and freshens with all the sweetness of valley and plain. Next comes the trembler-blade which governs the spark, and is in its turn controlled by the movement of the motor. The soul obeys what is properly the body, and the body, in most ingenious harmony, obeys the soul. But so strangely elastic is this preordained harmony that it is open to a more independent or more intelligent will—that of the driver, which stands here for the will of the gods—to improve still further this admirable equilibrium of two alien forces; and by means of the "advance ignition" lever, to precipitate the spark at the moment that the accidental aid or resistance of the road may render most favourable.

III

Let us pause for an instant to admire this strange terminology, so spontaneous and withal so sensible, which is, in a measure, the language of a new force. "Advance ignition," for instance, is a most adequate term, and we should find it vastly difficult to express more tersely and clearly what it was needful to say. The ignition is the inflammation of the explosive gases by the electric spark. And this explosion can be hastened or retarded in accordance with the requirements of the motor. When the "advance ignition" valve is opened, the spark springs forth some thousandth part of a second before the moment when it would logically produce itself; in other words, before the piston, attaining the end of its journey, shall have completely compressed the gas and utilized all the energy of the previous explosion. One would think, at first, that this premature explosion would counteract the ascending movement. Far from it; experience proves that one benefits by the infinitesimal time that the inflamed gases take to dilate themselves; as also probably by other causes no less obscure. In any event, we find that the pace of the machine is curiously accelerated. It is a device, like the glass of wine to the labourer, to procure a spell of abnormal strength. But whence does the term come, and who is its father? Whence do these words spring forth, at the given moment, to fix in life creatures of whose existence we were yesterday unaware? They escape from the factory, foundry or warehouse; they are the last echoes of that anonymous, universal voice that has given a name to trees and flowers, to bread and wine, to life and death; and fortunately it usually happens that by the time the pedant has begun to regard and question, it has become too late to make any change.

IV

Over and above such matters as compression, carburation, oiling, circulation of the water, etc., the trembler-blade and the sparking-plug are the driver's especial cares. Should the regulating screw of the one displace itself by the breadth of a hair, should the two opposed wires of the other be touched by a drop of oil or a trace of oxide, the miraculous horse will die on the spot. And around these are still many organs whereof I dare scarcely permit myself to think.

Yonder, concealed in its case, like a furious genie confined in a narrow cell, is the mysterious apparatus for the change of speed; and this, if you give a turn to the lever when you come to the foot of a hill, will produce repeated explosions, urging the piston to movement so frantic, that every vertebra of the creature will tremble and give to the slackening wheels a quadruple force before which each mountain will bend its back, and carry the conqueror humbly to its very crown. Further there is the enigmatic mechanism of the live axle which, dispensing with chains and straps, transmits directly to the two back wheels all the extraordinary power generated in its delirious heart. And still lower, beneath the brake, there rests, in its almost inviolable box, the transcendent secret of the *differentiator*, which, by means of a recent miracle, permits two wheels of the same dimensions, revolving on the same axle and moved by the same motor, to perform an unequal number of turns!

V

But at present I have no concern with these mighty mysteries. Beneath my tremulous hand the monster is alert and docile; and on either side of the road the cornfields flow peacefully onward, true rivers of green. The time has now come to try the power of esoteric action. I touch the magical handles. The fairy horse obeys. It stops abruptly. One short moan, and its life has all ebbed away. It is now nothing more than a vast, inert mass of metal. How to resuscitate it? I descend, and eagerly inspect the corpse. The plains, whose submissive immensity I have been braving, begin to contemplate revenge. Now that I have ceased to move, they fling themselves further and wider around me. The blue distance seems to recede, the sky to recoil. I am lost among the impassable cornfields, whose myriad heads press forward, whispering softly, craning to see what I am proposing to do; while the poppies, in the midst of that undulating crowd, nod their red caps and burst into thousandfold laughter. But no matter. My recent science is sure of itself. The hippogriff revives, gives its first snort of life, and then departs once more, singing its song. I reconquer the plains, which again bow down before me. I give a slow turn to the mysterious "advance ignition" lever, and regulate carefully the admission of the petrol. The pace grows faster and faster, the delirious wheels cry aloud in their gladness. And at first the road comes moving towards me, like a bride waving palms, rhythmically keeping time to some joyous melody. But soon it grows frantic, springs forward, and throws itself madly upon me, rushing under the car like a furious torrent, whose foam lashes my face; it drowns me beneath its waves, it blinds me with its breath. Oh, that wonderful breath! It is as though wings, as though myriad wings no eye can see, transparent wings of great supernatural birds that have their homes on invisible mountains swept by eternal snow, have come to refresh my eyes and my brow with their overwhelming fragrance! Now the road drops sheer into the abyss, and the magical carriage rushes ahead of it. The trees, that for so many slow-moving years have serenely dwelt on its borders, shrink back in dread of disaster. They seem to be hastening one to the other, to approach their green heads, and in startled groups to debate how to bar the way of the strange apparition. But as this rushes onward, they take panic, and scatter and fly, each one quickly seeking its own habitual place; and as I pass they bend tumultuously forward, and their myriad leaves, quick to the mad joy of the force that is chanting its hymn, murmur in my ears the voluble psalm of Space, acclaiming and greeting the enemy that hitherto has always been conquered but now at last triumphs: Speed.

VI

Space and Time, its invisible brother, are perhaps the two great enemies of mankind. Could we conquer these, we should be as the gods. Time seems invincible, having neither body nor form, no organs by which we can seize it. It passes, leaving traces that nearly always are sad, like the baleful shadow of some inevitable being we never have seen face to face. In itself doubtless it has no existence, but is only in relation to us; nor shall we ever succeed in bending to our will this necessary phantom of our organically false imagination. But Space, its magnificent brother, Space that decks itself with the green robe of the plains, the yellow veil of the desert, the blue mantle of the sea, and spreads over all the azure of the ether and the gold of the stars—Space, it may be, has already known many defeats; but never as yet has man seized it, as it were, round the body, grappled with it, alone, face to face. The monsters he has hitherto launched against its gigantic mass might conquer, but only to be conquered again in their turn.

On the sea great steamers subdue it day after day; but the sea is so vast that the extreme speed our frail lungs were able to endure could achieve no more than a kind of motionless triumph. And again, as we travel by rail, and Space flies submissive before us, it is still far away—we do not touch it, we do not enjoy it—it is like a captive adorning the triumph of a foreign king, and we ourselves the feeble prisoners of the power that has dethroned it. But here, in this little chariot of fire, that is so light and so docile, so gloriously untiring; here, beneath the unfolded wings of this bird of flame that flies low down over the earth in the midst of the flowers, greeting cornfields and rivulets, inviting the shade of the trees; passing village on village, glancing in at the open doors and watching the tables spread for the meal, counting the harvesters at work in the meadows, skirting the church, half hidden by lime-trees, and taking its rest at the inn on the stroke of noon—then setting forth once more, singing its song, to see at one bound what is happening among men at three days' march from the last place of halt, and surprising the very same hour in quite a new world—here Space does indeed become human, in the line of our eye, in accordance with the needs of our insatiable, exacting soul, that craves at once for the small and the mighty, the quick and the slow; here it is of us at last, it is ours, and offers at every turn glimpses of beauty that, in former days, we could only enjoy when the tedious journey was ended.

Now, however, it is not the arrival alone that causes our eyes to open, that revives the eagerness so precious to life, and invites admiration; now the entire road is one long succession of arrivals. The joys of the journey's end are multiplied, for all things adopt the admirable form of the end; the eyes are idle no longer, no longer indifferent; and memory, simplest of all the fairies whose touch of the wand brings happiness—memory, pondering silently on the less happy days that await every man, treasures the beauties of good mother earth; and fixes for ever, among those possessions of which none can deprive us, the unexpected gifts that have been so abundantly offered by the glad hours and the enfranchised roads.

NEWS OF SPRING

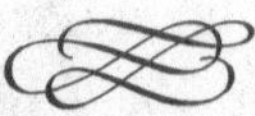

TRANSLATED BY ALEXANDER TEIXEIRA DE MATTOS.

I

I have seen the manner in which Spring stores up sunshine, leaves and flowers and makes ready, long beforehand, to invade the North. Here, on the ever-balmy shores of the Mediterranean—that motionless sea which looks as though it were under glass—where, while the months are dark in the rest of Europe, Spring has taken shelter from the wind and the snows in a palace of peace and light and love, it is interesting to detect its preparations for travelling in the fields of undying green. I can see clearly that it is afraid, that it hesitates once more to face the great frost-traps which February and March lay for it annually beyond the mountains. It waits, it dallies, it tries its strength before resuming the harsh and cruel way which the hypocrite Winter seems to yield to it. It stops, sets out again, revisits a thousand times, like a child running round the garden of its holidays, the fragrant valleys, the tender hills which the frost has never brushed with its wings. It has nothing to do here, nothing to revive, since nothing has perished and nothing suffered, since all the flowers of every season bathe here in the blue air of an eternal summer. But it seeks pretexts, it lingers, it loiters, it goes to and fro like an unoccupied gardener. It pushes aside the branches, fondles with its breath the olive-tree that quivers with a silver smile, polishes the glossy grass, rouses the corollas that were not asleep, recalls the birds that had never fled, encourages the bees that were workers without ceasing; and then, seeing, like God, that all is well in the spotless Eden, it rests for a moment on the ledge of a terrace which the orange-tree crowns with regular flowers and with fruits of light and, before leaving, casts a last look over its labour of joy and entrusts it to the sun.

II

I have followed it, these past few days, on the banks of the Borigo, from the torrent of Careï to the Val de Gorbio, in those little rustic towns, Ventimiglia, Tende, Sospello, in those curious villages, perched upon rocks, Sant' Agnese, Castellar, Castillon, in that adorable and already quite Italian country which surrounds Mentone. You go through a few streets quickened with the cosmopolitan and somewhat hateful life of the Riviera, you leave behind you the band-stand, with its everlasting town music, around which gather the consumptive rank and fashion of Mentone, and behold, at two steps from the crowd that dreads it as it would a scourge from Heaven, you find the admirable silence of the trees, all the goodly Virgilian realities of sunk roads, clear springs, shady pools that sleep on the mountain-sides, where they seem to await a goddess's reflection. You climb a path between two stone walls brightened by violets and crowned with the strange brown cowls of the arisarum, with its leaves of so deep a green that one might believe them to be created to symbolize the coolness of the well, and the amphitheatre of a valley opens like a moist and splendid flower. Through the blue veil of the giant olive-trees that cover the horizon with a transparent curtain of scintillating pearls, gleams the discreet and harmonious brilliancy of all that men imagine in their dreams and paint upon scenes that are thought unreal and unrealizable, when they wish to define the ideal gladness of an immortal hour, of some enchanted island, of a lost paradise, or the dwelling of the gods.

III

All along the valleys of the coast are hundreds of these amphitheatres which are as stages whereon, by moonlight or amid the peace of the mornings and afternoons, are acted the dumb fairy-plays of the world's contentment. They are all alike, and yet each of them reveals a different happiness. Each of them, as though they were the faces of a bevy of equally happy and equally beautiful sisters, wears its distinguishing smile. A cluster of cypresses, with its pure outline, a mimosa that resembles a bubbling spring of sulphur, a grove of orange-trees with dark and heavy tops symmetrically charged with golden fruits that suddenly proclaim the royal affluence of the soil that feeds them, a slope covered with lemon-trees, where the night seems to have heaped up on a mountain-side, to await a new twilight, the stars gathered by the dawn, a leafy portico which opens over the sea like a deep glance that suddenly discloses an infinite thought, a brook hidden like a tear of joy, a trellis awaiting the purple of the grapes, a great stone basin drinking in the water that trickles from the tip of a green reed: all and yet none modify the expression of the restfulness, the tranquillity, the azure silence, the blissfulness that is its own delight.

IV

But I am looking for Winter and the print of its footsteps. Where is it hiding? It should be here; and how dares this feast of roses and anemones, of soft air and dew, of bees and birds display itself with such assurance during the most pitiless month of Winter's reign? And what will Spring do, what will Spring say, since all seems done, since all seems said? Is it superfluous, then, and does nothing await it? No; search carefully: you shall find amid this life of unwearying youth the work of its hand, the perfume of its breath which is younger than life. Thus, there are foreign trees yonder, taciturn guests, like poor relations in ragged clothes. They come from very far, from the land of fog and frost and wind. They are aliens, sullen and distrustful. They have not yet learned the limpid speed, not adopted the delightful customs of the azure. They refused to believe in the promises of the sky and suspected the caresses of the sun which, from early dawn, covers them with a mantle of silkier and warmer rays than that with which July loaded their shoulders in the precarious summers of their native land. It made no difference: at the given hour, when snow was falling a thousand miles away, their trunks shivered, and, despite the bold averment of the grass and a hundred thousand flowers, despite the impertinence of the roses that climb up to them to bear witness to life, they stripped themselves for their winter sleep. Sombre and grim and bare as the dead, they await the Spring that bursts forth around them; and, by a strange and excessive reaction, they wait for it longer than under the harsh, gloomy sky of Paris, for it is said that in Paris the buds are already beginning to shoot. One catches glimpses of them here and there amid the holiday throng whose motionless dances enchant the hills. They are not many and they conceal themselves: they are gnarled oaks, beeches, planes; and even the vine, which one would have thought better-mannered, more docile and well-informed, remains incredulous. There they stand, black and gaunt, like sick people on an Easter Sunday in the church-porch made transparent by the splendour of the sun. They have been there for years and some of them, perhaps, for two or three centuries; but they have the terror of winter in their marrow. They will never lose the habit of death. They have too much experience, they are too old to forget and too old to learn. Their hardened reason refuses to admit the light when it does not come at the accustomed time. They are rugged old men, too wise to enjoy unforeseen pleasures. They are wrong. For here, around the old, around the grudging ancestors, is a whole world of plants that know nothing of the future, but give themselves to it. They live but for a season; they have no past and no traditions and they know nothing, except that the hour is fair and that they must enjoy it. While their elders, their masters and their gods, sulk and waste their time, they burst into flower; they love and they beget. They are the humble flowers of dear solitude: the Easter daisy that covers the sward with its frank and methodical neatness; the borage bluer than the bluest sky; the anemone, scarlet or dyed in aniline; the virgin primrose; the arborescent mallow; the bell-flower, shaking its bells that no one hears; the rosemary that looks like a little country maid; and the heavy thyme that thrusts its grey head between the broken stones.

But, above all, this is the incomparable hour, the diaphanous and liquid hour of the wood-violet. Its proverbial humility becomes usurping and almost intolerant. It no longer cowers timidly among the leaves: it hustles the grass, overtowers it, blots it out, forces its colours upon it, fills it with its breath. Its unnumbered smiles cover the terraces of olives and vines, the tracks of the ravines, the bend of the valleys with a net of sweet and innocent gaiety; its perfume, fresh and pure as the soul of the mountain spring, makes the air more translucent, the silence more limpid and is, in very deed, as a forgotten legend tells us, the breath of Earth, all bathed in dew, when, a virgin yet, she wakes in the sun and yields herself wholly in the first kiss of early dawn.

V

Again, in the little gardens that surround the cottages, the bright little houses with their Italian roofs, the good vegetables, unprejudiced and unpretentious, have known no fear. While the old peasant, who has come to resemble the trees he cultivates, digs the earth around the olives, the spinach assumes a lofty bearing, hastens to grow green nor takes the smallest precaution; the garden bean opens its eyes of jet in its pale leaves and sees the night fall unmoved; the fickle peas shoot and lengthen out, covered with motionless and tenacious butterflies, as though June had entered the farm-gate; the carrot blushes as it faces the light; the ingenuous strawberry-plants inhale the flavours which noontide lavishes upon them as it bends towards earth its sapphire urns; the lettuce exerts itself to achieve a heart of gold wherein to lock the dews of morning and night.

The fruit-trees alone have long reflected: the example of the vegetables among which they live urged them to join in the general rejoicing, but the rigid attitude of their elders from the North, of the grandparents born in the great dark forests, preached prudence to them. But now they awaken: they too can resist no longer and at last make up their minds to join the dance of perfumes and of love. The peach-trees are now no more than a rosy miracle, like the softness of a child's skin turned into azure vapour by the breath of dawn. The pear and plum and apple and almond-trees make dazzling efforts in drunken rivalry; and the pale hazel-trees, like Venetian chandeliers, resplendent with a cascade of gems, stand here and there to light the feast. As for the luxurious flowers that seem to possess no other object than themselves, they have long abandoned the endeavour to solve the mystery of this boundless summer. They no longer score the seasons, no longer count the days, and, knowing not what to do in the glowing disarray of hours that have no shadow, dreading lest they should be deceived and lose a single second that might be fair, they have resolved to bloom without respite from January to December. Nature approves them and, to reward their trust in happiness, their generous beauty and amorous excesses, grants them a force, a brilliancy and perfumes which she never gives to those which hang back and show a fear of life.

All this, among other truths, was proclaimed by the little house that I saw to-day on the side of a hill all deluged in roses, carnations, wall-flowers, heliotrope and mignonette, so as to suggest the source, choked and overflowing with flowers, whence Spring was preparing to pour down upon us; while, upon the stone threshold of the closed door, pumpkins, lemons, oranges, limes and Turkey figs slumbered in the majestic, deserted, monotonous silence of a perfect day.

THE WRATH OF THE BEE

TRANSLATED BY ALEXANDER TEIXEIRA DE MATTOS.

I

Since the publication of "The Life of the Bee," I have often been asked to throw light upon one of the most dreaded mysteries of the hive, namely, the psychology of its inexplicable, sudden and sometimes mortal wrath. A crowd of cruel and unjust legends, in fact, hovers around the abode of the yellow fairies of the honey. The bravest among the guests who visit the garden slacken their pace and lapse into involuntary silence as they approach the enclosure, blooming with clover and mignonette, where buzz the daughters of the light. Doting mothers keep their children away from it, as they would keep them away from a smouldering fire or a nest of adders; nor does the bee-keeping novice, gloved in leather, veiled in gauze, surrounded by clouds of smoke, face the mystic citadel without that little unavowed shiver which men feel before a great battle.

How much reason is there at the bottom of these traditional

fears? Is the bee really dangerous? Does she allow herself to be tamed? Is there a risk in approaching the hives? Ought we to flee or to face their wrath? Has the bee-keeper some secret or some talisman that preserves him from being stung? These are the questions that are anxiously put by all those who have started a timid hive and who are beginning their apprenticeship.

II

The bee, in general, is neither ill-disposed nor aggressive, but appears somewhat capricious. She has an unconquerable antipathy to certain people; she also has days of enervation—for instance, when a storm is at hand—on which she shows herself extremely irritable. She has a most subtle and susceptible sense of smell; she tolerates no perfume and detests, above all, the scent of human sweat and of alcohol. She is not to be tamed, in the proper sense of the word; but, whereas the hives which we seldom visit become crabbed and distrustful, those which we surround with our daily cares soon grow accustomed to the discreet and prudent presence of man. Lastly, to enable us to handle the bees almost without impunity, there exist a certain number of little expedients which vary according to circumstances and which can be learnt by practice alone. But it is time to reveal the great secret of their wrath.

III

The bee, essentially so pacific, so long-suffering, the bee, which never stings (unless you crush her) when looting among the flowers, once she has returned to her kingdom with the waxen monuments, retains her mild and tolerant character, or grows violent and deadly dangerous, according as her maternal city be opulent or poor. Here again, as often happens when we study the manners of this spirited and mysterious little people, the provisions of human logic are utterly at fault. It would be natural that the bees should defend desperately treasures so laboriously amassed, a city such as we find in good apiaries, where the nectar, overflowing the numberless cells that represent thousands of casks piled from cellar to garret, streams in golden stalactites along the rustling walls and sends far afield, in glad response to the ephemeral perfumes of calyces that are opening, the more lasting perfume of the honey that keeps alive the memory of calyces which time has closed. Now this is not the case. The richer their abode, the less eagerness they display to fight around it. Open or turn over a wealthy hive; if you take care to drive the sentries from the entrance with a puff of smoke, it will be extremely rare for the other bees to contend with you for the liquid booty conquered from the smiles, from all the charms of the beautiful azure months. Try the experiment; I promise you impunity, if you touch only the heavier hives. You can turn them over and empty them; those throbbing flagons are perfectly harmless. What does it mean? Have the fierce amazons lost courage? Has abundance unnerved them, and have they, after the manner of the too fortunate inhabitants of luxurious towns, delegated the dangerous duties to the unhappy mercenaries who keep watch at the gates? No, it has never been observed that the greatest good fortune relaxes the valour of the bee. On the contrary, the more the republic prospers, the more harshly and severely are its laws applied, and the worker in a hive where superfluity accumulates labours much more zealously than her sister in an indigent hive. There are other reasons which we cannot wholly fathom, but which are likely reasons, if only we take into account the wild interpretation which the poor bee must needs place upon our monstrous doings. Seeing suddenly her huge dwelling-place upheaved, overturned, half-opened, she probably imagines that an inevitable, a natural catastrophe is occurring against which it were madness to struggle. She no longer resists, but neither does she flee. Admitting the ruin, it looks as though already, in her instinct, she saw the future dwelling which she hopes to build with the materials taken from the gutted town. She leaves the present defenceless in order to save the hereafter. Or else, perhaps, does she, like the dog in the fable, "the dog that carried his master's dinner round his neck," knowing that all is irreparably lost, prefer to die taking her share of the pillage and to pass from life to death in one prodigious orgy? We do not know for certain. How should we penetrate the motives of the bee, when those of the simplest actions of our brothers are beyond our ken?

IV

Still, the fact is that, at each great proof to which the city is put, at each trouble that appears to the bees to possess an inevitable character, no sooner has the infatuation spread from one to the other among the densely quivering people than the bees fling themselves upon their combs, violently tear the sacred lids from the provisions for the winter, topple head foremost and plunge their whole bodies into the sweet-smelling vats, imbibe with long draughts the chaste wine of the flowers, gorge themselves with it, intoxicate themselves with it, till their bronze-ringed forms lengthen and distend like compressed leather bottles. Now the bee, when swollen with honey, can no longer curve her abdomen at the angle required to draw her sting. She becomes, so to speak, mechanically harmless from that moment. It is generally imagined that the beekeeper employs the fumigator to stun, to half-asphyxiate the warriors that gather their treasure in the blue and thus to effect an entrance by favour of a defenceless slumber into the palace of the innumerous sleeping amazons. This is a mistake: the smoke serves first to drive back the guardians of the threshold, who are ever on the alert and extremely quarrelsome; then, two or three puffs come to spread panic among the workers: the panic provokes the mysterious orgy, and the orgy helplessness. Thus is the fact explained that, with bare arms and unprotected face, one can open the most populous hives, examine their combs, shake off the bees, spread them at one's feet, heap them up, pour them out like grains of corn and quietly gather the honey, in the midst of the deafening cloud of ousted workers, without having to suffer a single sting.

V

But woe to whoso touches the poor hives! Keep away from the abodes of want! Here, smoke has lost its spell, and you shall scarce have emitted the first puffs before twenty thousand acrid and enraged demons will dart from within the walls, overwhelm your hands, blind your eyes and blacken your face. No living being, except, they say, the bear and the Sphinx Atropos, can resist the rage of the mailed legions. Above all, do not struggle: the fury would overtake the neighbouring colonies; and the smell of the spilt venom would enrage all the republics around. There is no means of safety other than instant flight through the bushes. The bee is less rancorous, less implacable than the wasp and rarely pursues her enemy. If flight be impossible, absolute immobility alone might calm her or put her off the scent. She fears and attacks any too sudden movement, but at once forgives that which no longer stirs.

The poor hives live, or rather die from day to day, and it is because they have no honey in their cellars that smoke makes no impression on them. They cannot gorge themselves like their sisters that belong to happier tribes; the possibilities of a future city are not there to divert their ardour. Their only thought is to perish on the outraged threshold, and, lean, shrunk, nimble, unrestrained, they defend it with unheard-of heroism and desperation. Therefore, the cautious beekeeper never displaces the indigent hives without making a preliminary sacrifice to the hungry Furies. His offering is a honey-comb. They come hastening up and then, the smoke assisting, they distend and intoxicate themselves: behold them reduced to helplessness like the rich burgesses of the plentiful cells.

VI

One could find much more to tell of the wrath of the bees and their singular antipathies. These antipathies are often so strange that they were for long attributed, that they are still attributed, by the peasants, to moral causes, to profound and mystic intuitions. There is the conviction, for instance, that the vestal vintagers cannot endure the approach of the unchaste, above all of the adulterous. It would be surprising if the most rational beings that live with us on this incomprehensible globe were to attach so much importance to a trespass that is often very harmless. In reality, they give it no thought; but they, whose whole life sways to the nuptial and sumptuous breath of the flowers, abhor the perfumes which we steal from them. Are we to believe that chastity exhales fewer odours than love? Is this the origin of the rancour of the jealous bees and of the legend that avenges virtues as jealous as they? Be this as it may, the legend must be classed with the many others that pretend to do great honour to the phenomena of nature by ascribing human feelings to them. It would be better, on the contrary, to mix our petty human psychology as little as possible with all that we do not easily understand, to seek our explanations only without, on this side of man or on that side; for it is probably there that lie the positive revelations which we are still awaiting.

FIELD FLOWERS

TRANSLATED BY ALEXANDER TEIXEIRA DE MATTOS.

I

They welcome our steps without the city gates, on a gay and eager carpet of many colours, which they wave madly in the sunlight. It is evident that they were expecting us. When the first bright rays of March appeared, the Snowdrop, or Amaryllis, the heroic daughter of the hoar-frost, sounded the reveille. Next sprang from the earth efforts, as yet shapeless, of a slumbering memory: vague ghosts of flowers; pale flowers that are scarcely flowers at all: the three-fingered Saxifrage, or Samphire; the almost invisible Shepherd's Pouch; the two-leaved Squill; the Stinking Hellebore, or Christmas Rose; the Colt's Foot; the gloomy and poisonous Spurge Laurel: all plants of frail and doubtful health, pale-blue, pale-pink, undecided attempts, the first fever of life in which nature expels her ill humours, anæmic captives set free by winter, convalescent patients from the underground prisons, timid and unskilful endeavours of the still buried light.

But soon this light ventures forth into space; the nuptial thoughts of the earth become clearer and purer; the rough attempts disappear; the half-dreams of the night lift like a fog dispelled by the dawn; and the good rustic flowers begin their unseen revels under the blue, all around the cities where man knows them not. No matter, they are there, making honey, while their proud and barren sisters, who alone receive our care, are still trembling in the depths of the hot-houses. They will still be there, in the flooded fields, in the broken paths, and adorning the roads with their simplicity, when the first snows shall have covered the country-side. No one sows them and no one gathers them. They survive their glory, and man treads them under foot. Formerly, however, and not so long ago, they alone represented Nature's gladness. Formerly, however, a few hundred years ago, before their dazzling and chilly kinswomen had come from the Antilles, from India, from Japan, or before their own daughters, ungrateful and unrecognizable, had usurped their place, they alone enlivened the stricken gaze, they alone brightened the cottage porch, the castle precincts, and followed the lovers' foot-steps in the woods. But those times are no more; and they are dethroned. They have retained of their past happiness only the names which they received when they were loved.

And these names show all that they were to man: all his grati-tude, his studious fondness, all that he owed them, all that they gave him are there contained, like a secular aroma in hollow pearls. And so they bear names of queens, shepherdesses, virgins, princesses, sylphs and fairies, which flow from the lips like a caress, a light-ning-flash, a kiss, a murmur of love. Our language, I think, contains nothing that is better, more daintily, more affectionately named than these homely flowers. Here the word clothes the idea almost always with care, with light precision, with admirable happiness. It is like an ornate and transparent stuff that moulds the form which it embraces and has the proper shade, perfume and sound. Call to mind the Easter Daisy, the Violet, the Bluebell, the Poppy, or, rather, Coquelicot: the name is the flower itself. How wonderful, for instance, that sort of cry and crest of light and joy: "Coquelicot!" to designate the scarlet flower which the scientists crush under this barbarous title: *Papaver rhœas!* See the Primrose, or, rather, the Cowslip, the Periwinkle, the Anemone, the Wild Hyacinth, the blue Speedwell, the Forget-me-not, the Wild Bindweed, the Iris, the Harebell: their name depicts them by equivalents and analogies which the greatest poets but rarely light upon. It represents all their ingenuous and visible soul. It hides itself, it bends over, it rises to the ear even as those who bear it lie concealed, stoop forward, or stand erect in the corn and in the grass.

These are the few names that are known to all of us; we do not know the others, though their music describes with the same gentleness, the same happy genius, flowers which we see by every wayside and upon all the paths. Thus, at this moment, that is to say, at the end of the month in which the ripe corn falls beneath the reaper's sickle, the banks of the roads are a pale violet: it is the Sweet Scabious, who has blossomed at last, discreet, aristocratically poor and modestly beautiful, as her title, that of a mist-veiled precious stone, proclaims. Around her, a treasure lies scattered: it is the Ranunculus, or Buttercup, who has two names, even as he has two lives; for he is at once the innocent virgin that covers the grass with sun-drops, and the redoubtable and venomous wizard that deals out death to heedless animals. Again we have the Milfoil and the St. John's Wort, little flowers, once useful, that march along the roads, like silent school-girls, clad in a dull uniform; the vulgar and innumerous Bird's Groundsel; her big brother, the Hare's Lettuce of the fields; then the dangerous black Nightshade; the Bitter-sweet, who hides herself; the creeping Knotweed, with the patient leaves: all the families without show, with the resigned smile, wearing the practical grey livery of autumn, which already is felt to be at hand.

II

But, among those of March, April, May, June, July, remember the glad and festive names, the springtime syllables, the vocables of azure and dawn, of moonlight and sunshine! Here is the Snowdrop, or Amaryllis, who proclaims the thaw; the Stitchwort, or Lady's Collar, who greets the first-communicants along the hedges, whose leaves are as yet indeterminate and uncertain, like a diaphanous green lye. Here are the sad Columbine and the Field Sage, the Jasione, the Angelica, the Field Fennel, the Wallflower, dressed like a servant of a village-priest; the Osmond, who is a king fern; the Luzula, the Parmelia, the Venus' Looking-glass; the Esula or Wood Spurge, mysterious and full of sombre fire; the Physalidis, whose fruit ripens in a lantern; the Henbane, the Belladonna, the Digitalis, poisonous queens, veiled Cleopatras of the untilled places and the cool woods. And then, again, the Camomile, the good-capped Sister with a thousand smiles, bringing the health-giving brew in an earth-enware bowl; the Pimpernel and the Coronilla, the pale Mint and the pink Thyme, the Sainfoin and the Euphrasy, the Ox-eye Daisy, the mauve Gentian and the blue Verbena, the Anthemis, the lance-shaped Horse-Thistle, the Cinquefoil or Potentilla, the Dyer's Weed ... to tell their names is to recite a poem of grace and light. We have reserved for them the most charming, the purest, the clearest sounds and all the musical gladness of the language. One would think that they were the persons of a play, dancers and choristers of an immense fairy-scene, more beautiful, more startling and more supernatural than the scenes that unfold themselves on Prospero's Island, at the Court of Theseus, or in the Forest of Arden. And the comely actresses of this silent, never-ending comedy—goddesses, angels, she-devils, princesses and witches, virgins and courtezans, queens and shepherd-girls—carry in the folds of their names the magic sheens of innumerous dawns, of innumerous springtimes contemplated by forgotten men, even as they also carry the memory of thousands of deep or fleeting emotions which were felt before them by generations that have disappeared, leaving no other trace.

III

They are interesting and incomprehensible. They are vaguely called the "Weeds." They serve no purpose. Here and there, a few, in very old villages, retain the spell of contested virtues. Here and there, one of them, right at the bottom of the apothecary's or herbalist's jars, still awaits the coming of the sick man faithful to the infusions of tradition. But sceptic medicine will have none of them. No longer are they gathered according to the olden rites; and the science of "Simples" is dying out in the housewife's memory. A merciless war is waged upon them. The husbandman fears them; the plough pursues them; the gardener hates them and has armed himself against them with clashing weapons: the spade and the rake, the hoe and the scraper, the weeding-hook, the grubbing-axe. Along the high-roads, their last refuge, the passerby crushes them, the waggon bruises them. In spite of all, they are there: permanent, assured, abundant, peaceful; and not one but answers the summons of the sun. They follow the seasons without swerving by an hour. They take no account of man, who exhausts himself in conquering them, and, so soon as he rests, they spring up in his footsteps. They live on, audacious, immortal, untamable. They have peopled our flower-baskets with extravagant and unnatural daughters; but they, the poor mothers, have remained similar to what they were a hundred thousand years ago. They have not added a fold to their petals, reordered a pistil, altered a shade, invented a perfume. They keep the secret of a mysterious mission. They are the indelible primitives. The soil is theirs since its origin. They represent, in short, an essential smile, an invariable thought, an obstinate desire of the Earth.

That is why it is well to question them. They have evidently something to tell us. And, then, let us not forget that they were the first—with the sunrises and sunsets, with the springs and autumns, with the song of the birds, with the hair, the glance and the divine movements of women—to teach our fathers that there are useless and beautiful things upon this globe.

CHRYSANTHEMUMS

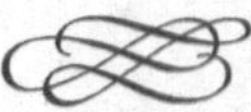

TRANSLATED BY ALEXANDER TEIXEIRA DE MATTOS.

I

Every year, in November, at the season that follows on the hour of the dead, the crowning and majestic hour of autumn, reverently I go to visit the chrysanthemums in the places where chance offers them to my sight. For the rest, it matters little where they are shown to me by the good will of travel or of sojourn. They are, indeed, the most universal, the most diverse of flowers; but their diversity and surprises are, so to speak, concerted, like those of fashion, in I know not what arbitrary Edens. At the same moment, even as with silks, laces, jewels and curls, a mysterious voice gives the pass-word in time and space; and, docile as the most beautiful women, simultaneously, in every country, in every latitude, the flowers obey the sacred decree.

It is enough, then, to enter at random one of those crystal museums in which their somewhat funereal riches are displayed under the harmonious veil of the days of November. We at once grasp the dominant idea, the obtrusive beauty, the unexpected effort of the year in this special world, strange and privileged even in the midst of the strange and privileged world of flowers. And we ask ourselves if this new idea is a profound and really necessary idea on the part of the sun, the earth, life, autumn, or man.

II

Yesterday, then, I went to admire the year's gentle and gorgeous floral feast, the last which the snows of December and January, like a broad belt of peace, sleep, silence and night, separate from the delicious festivals that commence again with the germination (powerful already, though hardly visible) that seeks the light in February.

They are there, under the immense transparent dome, the noble flowers of the month of fogs; they are there, at the royal meeting-place, all the grave little autumn fairies, whose dances and attitudes seem to have been struck motionless with a single word. The eye that recognizes them and has learned to love them perceives, at the first pleased glance, that they have actively and dutifully continued to evolve towards their uncertain ideal. Go back for a moment to their modest origin: look at the poor buttercup of yore, the humble little crimson or damask rose that still smiles sadly, along the roads full of dead leaves, in the scanty garden-patches of our villages; compare with them these enormous masses and fleeces of snow, these disks and globes of red copper, these spheres of old silver, these trophies of alabaster and amethyst, this delirious prodigy of petals which seems to be trying to exhaust to its last riddle the world of autumnal shapes and shades which the winter entrusts to the bosom of the sleeping woods; let the unwonted and unexpected varieties pass before your eyes; admire and appraise them.

Here, for instance, is the marvellous family of the stars: flat stars, bursting stars, diaphanous stars, solid and fleshly stars, milky ways and constellations of the earth that correspond with those of the firmament. Here are the proud plumes that await the diamonds of the dew; here, to put our dreams to shame, the fascinating poem of unreal tresses: wise, precise and meticulous tresses; mad and miraculous tresses; honeyed moonbeams, golden bushes and flaming whirlpools; curls of fair and smiling maidens, of fleeing nymphs, of passionate bacchantes, of swooning sirens, of cold virgins, of frolicsome children, whom angels, mothers, fauns, lovers have caressed with their calm or quivering hands. And then, here, pell-mell, are the monsters that cannot be classed: hedgehogs, spiders, curly endives, pine-apples, pompons, Tudor roses, shells, vapours, breaths, stalactites of ice and falling snow, a throbbing hail of sparks, wings, flashes, fluffy, pulpy, fleshy things, wattles, bristles, funeral piles and sky-rockets, bursts of light, a stream of fire and sulphur.

III

Now that the shapes have capitulated comes the question of conquering the region of the proscribed colours, of the reserved shades, which the autumn, as we can see, denies to the flowers that represent it. Lavishly it bestows on them all the wealth of the twilight and the night, all the riches of the harvest-time: it gives them all the mud-brown work of the rain in the woods, all the silvery fashionings of the mist in the plains, of the frost and the snow in the gardens. It permits them, above all, to draw at will upon the inexhaustible treasures of the dead leaves and the expiring forest. It allows them to deck themselves with the golden sequins, the bronze medals, the silver buckles, the copper spangles, the elfin plumes, the powdered amber, the burnt topazes, the neglected pearls, the smoked amethysts, the calcined garnets, all the dead but still dazzling jewellery which the North Wind heaps up in the hollows of ravines and foot-paths; but it insists that they shall remain faithful to their old masters and wear the livery of the drab and weary months that give them birth. It does not permit them to betray those masters and to don the princely, changing dresses of the spring and the dawn; and, if, sometimes, it suffers a pink, this is only on condition that it be borrowed from the cold lips, the pale brow of the veiled and afflicted virgin praying on a tomb. It forbids most strictly the tints of summer, of too youthful, ardent and serene a life, of a health too joyous and expansive. In no case will it consent to hilarious vermilions, impetuous scarlets, imperious and dazzling purples. As for the blues, from the azure of the dawn to the indigo of the sea and the deep lakes, from the periwinkle to the borage and the corn-flower, they are banished on pain of death.

IV

Nevertheless, thanks to some forgetfulness of nature, the most unusual colour in the world of flowers and the most severely forbidden—the colour which the corolla of the poisonous euphorbia is almost the only one to wear in the city of the umbels, petals and calyces—green, the colour exclusively reserved for the servile and nutrient leaves, has penetrated within the jealously-guarded precincts. True, it has slipped in only by favour of a lie, as a traitor, a spy, a livid deserter. It is a forsworn yellow, steeped fearfully in the fugitive azure of the moonbeam. It is still of the night and false, like the opal depths of the sea; it reveals itself only in shifting patches at the tips of the petals; it is vague and anxious, frail and elusive, but undeniable. It has made its entrance, it exists, it asserts itself; it will be daily more fixed and more determined; and, through the breach which it has contrived, all the joys and all the splendours of the banished prism will hurl themselves into their virgin domain, there to prepare unaccustomed feasts for our eyes. This is a great tiding and a memorable conquest in the land of flowers.

We must not think that it is puerile thus to interest one's self in the capricious forms, the unwritten shades of a humble, useless flower, nor must we treat those who seek to make it more beautiful or more strange as La Bruyère once treated the lover of the tulip or the plum. Do you remember the charming page?

"The lover of flowers has a garden in the suburbs, where he spends all his time from sunrise to sunset. You see him standing there and would think that he had taken root in the midst of his tulips before his 'Solitaire;' he opens his eyes wide, rubs his hands, stoops down and looks closer at it; it never before seemed to him so handsome; he is in an ecstasy of joy, and leaves it to go to the 'Orient,' then to the 'Widow,' from thence to the 'Cloth of Gold,' on to the 'Agatha,' and at last returns to the 'Solitaire,' where he remains, is tired out, sits down, and forgets his dinner; he looks at the tulip and admires its shade, shape, colour, sheen and edges, its beautiful form and calyc; but God and nature are not in his thoughts, for they do not go beyond the bulb of his tulip, which he would not sell for a thousand crowns, though he will give it to you for nothing when tulips are no longer in fashion and carnations are all the rage. This rational being, who has a soul and professes some religion, comes home tired and half starved, but very pleased with his day's work: he has seen some tulips.

"Talk to another of the healthy look of the crops, of a plentiful harvest, of a good vintage, and you will find that he cares only for fruit and understands not a single word that you say; then turn to figs and melons; tell him that this year the pear-trees are so heavily laden with fruit that the branches almost break, that there are abundance of peaches, and you address him in a language which he completely ignores, and he will not answer you, for his sole hobby is plum-trees. Do not even speak to him of your plum-trees, for he is fond of only a certain kind and laughs and sneers at the mention of any others; he takes you to his tree and cautiously gathers this exquisite plum, divides it, gives you one half, keeps the other himself and exclaims, 'How delicious! Do you like it? Is it not heavenly? You cannot find its equal anywhere;' and then his nostrils dilate, and he can hardly contain his joy and pride under an appearance of modesty. What a wonderful person, never enough praised and admired, whose name will be handed down to future ages! Let me look at his mien and shape, while he is still in the land of the living, that I may study the features and the countenance of a man who, alone among mortals, is the happy possessor of such a plum."

Well, La Bruyère is wrong. We readily forgive him his mistake, for the sake of the marvellous window, which he, alone among the authors of his time, opens upon the unexpected gardens of the seventeenth century. The fact none the less remains that it is to his somewhat bigoted florist, to his somewhat frenzied horticulturist that we owe our exquisite flower-beds, our more varied, more abundant, more luscious vegetables, our even more delicious fruits. Contemplate, for instance, around the chrysanthemums, the marvels that ripen nowadays in the meanest gardens, among the long branches wisely subdued by the patient and generous espaliers. Less than a century ago, they were unknown; and we owe them to the trifling and innumerable exertions of a legion of small seekers, all more or less narrow, all more or less ridiculous.

It is thus that man acquires nearly all his riches. There is nothing that is puerile in nature; and he who becomes impassioned of a flower, a blade of grass, a butterfly's wing, a nest, a shell, wraps his passion around a small thing that always contains a great truth. To succeed in modifying the appearance of a flower is insignificant in itself, if you will; but reflect upon it for however short a while, and it becomes gigantic. Do we not violate, or deviate, profound, perhaps essential and, in any case, time-honoured laws? Do we not exceed too easily accepted limits? Do we not directly intrude our ephemeral will on that of the eternal forces? Do we not give the idea of a singular power, a power almost supernatural, since it inverts a natural order of things? And, although it is prudent to guard against over-ambitious dreams, does not this allow us to hope that we may perhaps learn to elude or to transgress other laws no less time-honoured, nearer to ourselves and important in a very different manner? For, in short, all things touch, all things go hand to hand; all things obey the same invisible principles, the identical exigencies; all things share in the same spirit, in the same substance, in the terrifying and wonderful problem; and the most modest victory gained in the matter of a flower may one day disclose to us an infinity of the untold....

V

Because of these things I love the chrysanthemum; because of these things I follow its evolution with a brother's interest. It is, among familiar plants, the most submissive, the most docile, the most tractable and the most attentive plant of all that we meet on life's long way. It bears flowers impregnated through and through with the thought and will of man: flowers already human, so to speak. And, if the vegetable world is some day to reveal to us one of the words that we are awaiting, perhaps it will be through this flower of the tombs that we shall learn the first secret of existence, even as, in another kingdom, it is probably through the dog, the almost thinking guardian of our homes, that we shall discover the mystery of animal life.

OLD-FASHIONED FLOWERS

TRANSLATED BY ALEXANDER TEIXEIRA DE MATTOS.

I

This morning, when I went to look at my flowers, surrounded by their white fence, which protects them against the good cattle grazing in the field beyond, I saw again in my mind all that blossoms in the woods, the fields, the gardens, the orangeries and the green-houses and I thought of all that we owe to the world of marvels which the bees visit.

Can we conceive what humanity would be if it did not know the flowers? If these did not exist, if they had all been hidden from our gaze, as are probably a thousand no less fairy sights that are all around us, but invisible to our eyes, would our character, our faculties, our sense of the beautiful, our aptitude for happiness be quite the same? We should, it is true, in nature have other splendid manifestations of luxury, exuberance and grace; other dazzling efforts of the superfluous forces: the sun, the stars, the varied lights of the moon, the azure and the ocean, the dawns and twilights, the mountain, the plain, the forest and the rivers, the light and the trees and, lastly, nearer to us, birds, precious stones and woman. These are the ornaments of our planet. Yet, but for the last three, which belong to the same smile of nature, how grave, austere, almost sad would be the education of our eye, without the softness which the flowers give! Suppose for a moment that our globe knew them not: a great region, the most enchanted in the joys of our psychology, would be destroyed, or rather would not be discovered. All of a delightful sense would sleep for ever at the bottom of our harder and more desert hearts and in our imagination stripped of worshipful images. The infinite world of colours and shades would have been but incompletely revealed to us by a few rents in the sky. The miraculous harmonies of light at play, ceaselessly inventing new gaieties, revelling in itself, would be unknown to us; for the flowers first broke up the prism and made the most subtle portion of our sight. And the magic garden of perfumes: who would have opened its gate to us? A few grasses, a few gums, a few fruits, the breath of the dawn, the smell of the night and the sea would have told us that beyond our eyes and ears there existed a shut paradise where the air which we breathe changes into delights for which we could have found no name. Consider also all that the voice of human happiness would lack! One of the blessed heights of our soul would be almost dumb, if the flowers had not, since centuries, fed with their beauty the language which we speak and the thoughts that endeavour to crystallize the most precious hours of life. The whole vocabulary, all the impressions of love, are impregnate with their breath, nourished with their smile. When we love, all the flowers that we have seen and smelt seem to hasten within us to people with their known charms the consciousness of a sentiment whose happiness, but for them, would have no more form than the horizons of the sea or sky. They have accumulated within us, since our childhood, and even before it, in the soul of our fathers, an immense treasure, the nearest to our joys, upon which we draw each time that we wish to make more real the clement minutes of our life. They have created and spread in our world of sentiment the fragrant atmosphere in which love delights.

II

That is why I love above all the simplest, the commonest, the oldest and the most antiquated; those which have a long human past behind them, a large array of kind and consoling actions; those which have lived with us for hundreds of years and which form part of ourselves, since they reflect something of their grace and their joy of life in the soul of our ancestors.

But where do they hide themselves? They are becoming rarer than those which we call rare flowers to-day. Their life is secret and precarious. It seems as though we were on the point of losing them, and perhaps there are some which, discouraged at last, have lately disappeared, of which the seeds have died under the ruins, which will no more know the dew of the gardens and which we shall find only in very old books, amid the bright grass of the Illuminators or along the yellow flower-beds of the Primitives.

They are driven from the borders and the proud baskets by arrogant strangers from Peru, the Cape of Good Hope, China, Japan. They have two pitiless enemies in particular. The first of these is the encumbering and prolific Begonia Tuberosa, that swarms in the beds like a tribe of turbulent fighting-cocks, with innumerous combs. It is pretty, but insolent and a little artificial; and, whatever the silence and meditation of the hour, under the sun and under the moon, in the intoxication of the day and the solemn peace of the night, it sounds its clarion cry and celebrates its victory, monotonous, shrill and scentless. The other is the Double Geranium, not quite so indiscreet, but indefatigable also and extraordinarily courageous. It would appear desirable were it less lavished. These two, with the help of a few more cunning strangers and of the plants with coloured leaves that close up those turgid mosaics which at present debase the beautiful lines of most of our lawns, these two have gradually ousted their native sisters from the spots which these had so long brightened with their familiar smiles. They no longer have the right to receive the guest with artless little cries of welcome at the gilded gates of the mansion. They are forbidden to prattle near the steps, to twitter in the marble vases, to hum their tune beside the lakes, to lisp their dialect along the borders. A few of them have been relegated to the kitchen-garden, in the neglected and, for that matter, delightful corner occupied by the medicinal or merely aromatic plants, the Sage, the Tarragon, the Fennel and the Thyme, old servants, too, dismissed and nourished through a sort of pity or mechanical tradition. Others have taken refuge by the stables, near the low door of the kitchen or the cellar, where they crowd humbly like importunate beggars, hiding their bright dresses among the weeds and holding their frightened perfumes as best they may, so as not to attract attention.

But, even there, the Pelargonium, red with indignation, and the Begonia, crimson with rage, came to surprise and hustle the unoffending little band; and they fled to the farms, the cemeteries, the little gardens of the rectories, the old maid's houses and the country convents. And now hardly anywhere, save in the oblivion of the oldest villages, around tottering dwellings, far from the railways and the nursery-gardener's overbearing hot-houses, do we find them again with their natural smile: not wearing a driven, panting and hunted look, but peaceful, calm, restful, plentiful, careless and at home. And, even as in former times, in the coaching-days, from the top of the stone wall that surrounds the house, through the rails of the white fence, or from the sill of the windows enlivened by a caged bird, on the motionless road where none passes, save the eternal forces of life, they see spring come and autumn, the rain and the sun, the butterflies and the bees, the silence and the night followed by the light of the moon.

III

Brave old flowers! Wall-flowers, Gilly-flowers, Stocks! For, even as the field-flowers, from which a trifle, a ray of beauty, a drop of perfume, divides them, they have charming names, the softest in the language; and each of them, like tiny, artless ex-votos, or like medals bestowed by the gratitude of men, proudly bears three or four. You Stocks, who sing among the ruined walls and cover with light the grieving stones, you Garden Primroses, Primulas or Cowslips, Hyacinths, Crocuses, Crown Imperials, Scented Violets, Lilies of the Valley, Forget-me-nots, Daisies and Periwinkles, Poet's Narcissuses, Pheasant's Eyes, Bear's Ears, Alyssums, Saxifrage, Anemones: it is through you that the months that come before the leaf-time—February, March, April—translate into smiles which men can understand the first news and the first mysterious kisses of the sun! You are frail and chilly and yet as bold-faced as a bright idea. You make young the grass; you are fresh as the water that flows in the azure cups which the dawn distributes over the greedy buds, ephemeral as the dreams of a child, almost wide still and almost spontaneous, yet already marked by the too-precocious brilliancy, the too-flaming nimbus, the too-pensive grace that overwhelm the flowers which yield obedience to man.

IV

But here, innumerous, disordered, many-coloured, tumultuous, drunk with dawns and noons, come the luminous dances of the daughters of Summer! Little girls with white veils and old maids in violet ribbons, school-girls home for the holidays, first-communicants, pale nuns, dishevelled romps, gossips and prudes. Here is the Marigold, who breaks up with her brightness the green of the borders. Here is the Camomile, like a nosegay of snow, beside her unwearying brothers, the Garden Chrysanthemums, whom we must not confuse with the Japanese Chrysanthemums of autumn. The Annual Helianthus, or Sunflower, towers like a priest raising the monstrance over the lesser folk in prayer and strives to resemble the luminary which he adores. The Poppy exerts himself to fill with light his cup torn by the morning wind. The rough Larkspur, in his peasant's blouse, who thinks himself more beautiful than the sky, looks down upon the Dwarf Convolvuluses, who reproach him spitefully with putting too much blue into the azure of his flowers. The Virginia Stock, arch and demure in her gown of jaconet, like the little servant-maids of Dordrecht or Leyden, washes the borders of the beds with innocence. The Mignonette hides herself in her laboratory and silently distils perfumes that give us a foretaste of the air which we breathe on the threshold of Paradise. The Peonies, who have drunk their imprudent fill of the sun, burst with enthusiasm and bend forward to meet the coming apoplexy. The Scarlet Flax traces a blood-stained furrow that guards the walks; and the Portulaca, creeping like a moss, studies to cover with mauve, amber or pink taffeta the soil that has remained bare at the foot of the tall stalks. The chub-faced Dahlia, a little round, a little stupid, carves out of soap, lard or wax his regular pompons, which will be the ornament of a village holiday. The old, paternal Phlox, standing amid the clusters, lavishes the loud laughter of his jolly, easygoing colours. The Mallows, or Lavateras, like demure misses, feel the tenderest blushes of fugitive modesty mount to their corollas at the slightest breath. The Nasturtium paints his water colours, or screams like a parakeet climbing up the bars of its cage; and the Rose-mallow, Althæa Rosea, Hollyhock, riding the high horse of her many names, flaunts her cockades of a flesh silkier than a maiden's breast. The Snapdragon and the almost transparent Balsam are more timorous and awkward and fearfully press their flowers against their stalks.

Next, in the discreet corner of the old families, are crowded the long-leaved Veronica; the red Potentilla; the African Marigold; the ancient Lychnis, or Maltese Cross; the Mournful Widow, or Purple Scabious; the Foxglove, or Digitalis, who shoots up like a melancholy rocket; the European Aquilegia, or Columbine; the Viscaria, who, on a long, slim neck, lifts a small, ingenuous, quite round face to admire the sky; the lurking Lunaria, who secretly manufactures the "Pope's money," those pale, flat crown-pieces with which, no doubt, the elves and fairies by moonlight carry on their trade in spells; lastly, the Pheasant's Eye, the red Valerian, or Jupiter's Beard, the Sweet William and the old Carnation, that was cultivated long ago by the Grand Condé in his exile.

Besides these, above, all around, on the walls, in the hedges, among the arbours, along the branches, like a people of sportive monkeys and birds, the climbing plants make merry, perform feats of gymnastics, play at swinging, at losing and recovering their balance, at falling, at flying, at looking up at space, at reaching beyond the treetops to kiss the sky. Here we have the Spanish Bean and the Sweet Pea, quite proud at being no longer included among the vegetables; the modest Volubilis; the Honeysuckle, whose scent represents the soul of the dew; the Clematis and the Glycine; while, at the windows, between the white curtains, along the stretched string, the Campanula, surnamed Pyramidalis, works such miracles, throws out sheaves and twists garlands formed of a thousand uniform flowers so prodigiously immaculate and transparent that they who see it for the first time, refusing to believe their eyes, want to touch with their finger the bluey marvel, cool as a fountain, pure as a source, unreal as a dream.

Meanwhile, in a blaze of light, the great white Lily, the old lord of the gardens, the only authentic prince among all the commonalty issuing from the kitchen-garden, the ditches, the copses, the pools and the moors, among the strangers come from none knows where, with his invariable six-petalled chalice of silver, whose nobility dates back to that of the gods themselves: the immemorial Lily raises his ancient sceptre, august, inviolate, which creates around it a zone of chastity, silence and light.

V

I have seen them, those whom I have named and as many whom I have forgotten, all thus collected in the garden of an old sage, the same that taught me to love the bees. They displayed themselves in beds and clusters, in symmetrical borders, ellipses, oblongs, quincunxes and lozenges, surrounded by box hedges, red bricks, earthenware tiles or brass chains, like precious matters contained in ordered receptacles similar to those which we find in the discoloured engravings that illustrate the works of the old Dutch poet, Jacob Cats. And the flowers were drawn up in rows, some according to their kinds, others according to their shapes and shades, while others, lastly, mingled, according to the happy chances of the wind and the sun, the most hostile and murderous colours, in order to show that nature acknowledges no dissonance and that all that lives creates its own harmony.

From its twelve rounded windows, with their shining panes,

their muslin curtains, their broad green shutters, the long, painted house, pink and gleaming as a shell, watched them wake at dawn and throw off the brisk diamonds of the dew and then close at night under the blue darkness that falls from the stars. One felt that it took an intelligent pleasure in this gentle, daily fairy-scene, itself solidly planted between two clear ditches that lost themselves in the distance of the immense pasturage dotted with motionless cows, while, by the roadside, a proud mill, bending forward like a preacher, made familiar signs with its paternal sails to the passers-by from the village.

VI

Has this earth of ours a fairer ornament of its hours of leisure than the care of flowers? It was beautiful to see thus collected for the pleasure of the eyes, around the house of my placid friend, the splendid throng that tills the light to win from it marvellous colours, honey and perfumes. He found there translated into visible joys, fixed at the gates of his house, the scattered, fleeting and almost intangible delights of summer: the voluptuous air, the clement nights, the emotional sunbeams, the glad hours, the confiding dawn, the whispering and mysterious azured space. He enjoyed not only their dazzling presence: he also hoped—probably unwisely, so deep and confused is that mystery—he also hoped, by dint of questioning them, to surprise, with their aid, I know not what secret law or idea of nature, I know not what private thought of the universe, which perhaps betrays itself in those ardent moments in which it strives to please other beings, to beguile other lives and to create beauty.

VII

Old flowers, I said. I was wrong; for they are not so old. When we study their history and investigate their pedigrees, we learn with surprise that most of them, down to the simplest and commonest, are new beings, freedmen, exiles, new-comers, visitors, foreigners. Any botanical treatise will reveal their origins. The Tulip, for instance (remember La Bruyère's "Solitary," "Oriental," "Agate," and "Cloth of Gold"), came from Constantinople in the sixteenth century. The Ranuncula, the Lunaria, the Maltese Cross, the Balsam, the Fuchsia, the African Marigold, or Tagetes Erecta, the Rose Campion, or Lychnis Coronaria, the two-coloured Aconite, the Amaranthus Caudatus, or Love-lies-bleeding, the Hollyhock and the Campanula Pyramidalis arrived at about the same time from the Indies, Mexico, Persia, Syria and Italy. The Pansy appears in 1613; the Yellow Alyssum in 1710; the Perennial Flax in 1775; the Scarlet Flax in 1819; the Purple Scabious in 1629; the Saxifraga Sarmentosa in 1771; the long-leaved Veronica in 1713; the Perennial Phlox is a little older. The Indian Pink made its entrance into our gardens about 1713. The Garden Pink is of modern date. The Portulaca did not make her appearance till 1828; the Scarlet Sage till 1822. The Ageratum, or Cœlestinum, now so plentiful and so popular, is not two centuries old. The Helichrysum, or Everlasting, is even younger. The Zinnia is exactly a centenarian. The Spanish Bean, a native of South America, and the Sweet Pea, an immigrant from Sicily, number a little over two hundred years. The Anthemis, whom we find in the least-known villages, has been cultivated only since 1699. The charming blue Lobelia of our borders came to us from the Cape of Good Hope at the time of the French Revolution. The China Aster, or Reine Marguerite, is dated 1731. The Annual or Drummond's Phlox, now so common, was sent over from Texas in 1835. The large-flowered Lavatera, who looks so confirmed a native, so simple a rustic, has blossomed in our gardens only since two centuries and a half; and the Petunia since some twenty lustres. The Mignonette, the Heliotrope—who would believe it?—are not two hundred years old. The Dahlia was born in 1802; and the Gladiolus is of yesterday.

VIII

What flowers, then, blossomed in the gardens of our fathers? Very few, no doubt, and very small and very humble, scarce to be distinguished from those of the roads, the fields and the glades. Before the sixteenth century, those gardens were almost bare; and, later, Versailles itself, the splendid Versailles, could have shown us only what is shown to-day by the poorest village. Alone, the Violet, the Garden Daisy, the Lily of the Valley, the Marigold, the Poppy, a few Crocuses, a few Irises, a few Colchicums, the Foxglove, the Valerian, the Larkspur, the Cornflower, the Clove, the Forget-me-not, the Gilly-flower, the Mallow, the Rose, still almost a Sweetbriar, and the great silver Lily, the spontaneous finery of our woods and of our snow-frightened, wind-frightened fields: these alone smiled upon our forefathers, who, for that matter, were unaware of their poverty. Man had not yet learnt to look around him, to enjoy the life of nature. Then came the Renascence, the great voyages, the discovery and invasion of the sunlight. All the flowers of the world, the successful efforts, the deep, inmost beauties, the joyful thoughts and wishes of the planet rose up to us, borne on a shaft of light that, in spite of its heavenly wonder, issued from our own earth. Man ventured forth from the cloister, the crypt, the town of brick and stone, the gloomy stronghold in which he had slept. He went down into the garden, which became peopled with azure, purple and perfumes, opened his eyes, astounded like a child escaping from the dreams of the night; and the forest, the plain, the sea and the mountains and, lastly, the birds and the flowers, that speak in the name of all a more human language which he already understood, greeted his awakening.

IX

Nowadays, perhaps, there are no more unknown flowers. We have found all or nearly all the forms which nature lends to the great dream of love, to the yearning for beauty that stirs within her bosom. We live, so to speak, in the midst of her tenderest confidences, of her most touching inventions. We take an unhoped-for part in the most mysterious festivals of the invisible force that animates us also. Doubtless, in appearance, it is a small thing that a few more flowers should adorn our beds. They only scatter a few impotent smiles along the paths that lead to the grave. It is none the less true that these are new and very real smiles, which were unknown to those who came before us; and this recently-discovered happiness spreads in every direction, even to the doors of the most wretched hovels. The good, the simple flowers are as happy and as gorgeous in the poor man's strip of garden as in the broad lawns of the great house, and they surround the cottage with the supreme beauty of the earth; for the earth has till now produced nothing more beautiful than the flowers. They have completed the conquest of the globe. Foreseeing the days when men shall at last have long and equal leisure, already they promise an equality in sane enjoyments. Yes, assuredly it is a small thing; and everything is a small thing, if we look at each of our little victories one by one. It is a small thing, too, in appearance, that we should have a few more thoughts in our heads, a new feeling at our hearts; and yet it is just that which slowly leads us where we hope to win.

After all, we have here a very real fact, namely, that we live in a world in which flowers are more beautiful and more numerous than formerly; and perhaps we have the right to add that the thoughts of men are more just and greedier of truth. The smallest joy gained and the smallest grief conquered should be marked in the Book of Humanity. It behoves us not to lose sight of any of the evidence that we are mastering the nameless powers, that we are beginning to handle some of the mysterious laws that govern the created, that we are making our planet all our own, that we are adorning our stay and gradually broadening the acreage of happiness and of beautiful life.

SINCERITY

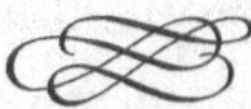

TRANSLATED BY ALEXANDER TEIXEIRA DE
MATTOS.

I

Love contains no complete and lasting happiness save in the transparent atmosphere of perfect sincerity. Until we attain this sincerity, our love is but an experiment: we live in expectation, and our words and kisses are only provisional. But sincerity is not possible except between lofty and trained consciences. Moreover, it is not enough that the consciences should be that: if sincerity is to become natural and essential, this is requisite besides, that the consciences shall be almost equal, of the same extent, of the same quality, and that the love that unites them shall be deep-laid. And thus it is that the lives glide away of so many men who never meet the soul with which they could have been sincere.

But it is impossible to be sincere with others before learning to be sincere with one's self. Sincerity is only the consciousness and analysis of the motives of all life's actions. It is the expression of this consciousness that one is able, later to lay before the eyes of the being with whom one is seeking the happiness of sincerity.

Thus understood, sincerity's aim is not to lead to moral perfection. It leads elsewhere, higher if we will: in any case to more human and more fertile regions. The perfection of a character, as we generally understand it, is too often but an unproductive abstention, a sort of ataraxy, an abatement of instinctive life which is, when all is said, the one source of all the other lives that we succeed in organizing within us. This perfection tends to suppress our too ardent desires: ambition, pride, vanity, egoism, the craving for enjoyment, in short, all the human passions, that is to say, all that constitutes our primitive vital force, the very groundwork of our energy of existence, which nothing can replace. If we stifle within ourselves all the manifestations of life, to substitute for them merely the contemplation of their defeat, soon we shall have nothing left to contemplate.

Wherefore, it is not of importance to have no more passions, vices or faults: that is impossible, so long as one is a man in the midst of men, since we make the mistake to describe as passion, vice or fault that which is the very basis of human nature. But it is of importance to recognize, in their details and in their secrets, those which we possess and to watch them at work from a standpoint so high that we may look upon them without fearing lest they should overthrow us or escape from our control to go and heedlessly to harm us or those around us.

So soon as, from that stand-point, we see our instincts, even the lowest and the most selfish, at work, provided that we are not wilfully wicked—and it is difficult to be that when our intelligence has acquired the lucidity and the force which this faculty of observation implies—so soon as we see them thus at work, they become harmless, like children under their parents' eyes. We can even lose sight of them, forget to watch them for a time; they will commit no serious misdeeds; for the obligation that lies upon them to repair the evil which they have done renders them naturally circumspect and soon makes them lose the habit of doing harm.

II

When we have achieved a sufficient sincerity with ourselves, it does not follow that we must deliver it to the first-comer. The frankest and most loyal man has the right to hide from others the greater part of what he thinks or feels. If it be uncertain whether the truth which you propose to speak will be understood, do not utter it. It would appear in others quite different from that which it is in you; and, taking in them the appearance of a lie, it would do the same harm as a real lie. Whatever the absolute moralists may say, so soon as one is no longer among equal consciences, every truth, to produce the effect of truth, requires focussing; and Jesus Christ Himself was obliged to focus the greater part of those which He revealed to His disciples, for, had He been addressing Plato or Seneca instead of speaking to fishers of Galilee, He would probably have said to them things different from those which He did say.

It is, therefore, right that we should present to each man only the truth for which he has room in the hut or the palace which he has built to admit the truths of his life. But let us, nevertheless, give ten or twenty times as many truths as we are offered in exchange; for in this, as in all circumstances, it behoves the more conscient to take the lead.

The reign of instinct begins only when this focussing is no longer necessary. We then enter the privileged region of confidence and love, which is like a delightful shore where we meet in our nakedness and bathe together under the rays of a kindly sun. Until this hour, man had lived on his guard, like a culprit. He did not yet know that every man has the right to be what he is; that there is no shame in his mind or in his heart, any more than in his body. He soon learns, with the feeling of relief of an acquitted prisoner, that that which he thought it his duty to conceal is just the most radical portion of the force of life. He is no longer alone in the mystery of his conscience; and the most pitiful secrets which he discovers there, far from saddening him as of yore, cause him to love better the firm and gentle light which two united hands turn upon it in concert.

All the evil, all the meannesses, all the weaknesses which we thus disclose in ourselves change their nature so soon as they are disclosed; "and the greatest fault," as the heroine of a recent drama says, "when confessed in a loyal kiss, becomes a truth more beautiful than innocence." More beautiful? I do not know; but younger, more vivid, more visible, more active and more loving.

In this state, the idea no longer comes to us to hide a secret thought or a secret sentiment, however vulgar or contemptible. They can no longer make us blush, seeing that, in owning them, we disown them, we separate them from ourselves, we prove that they no longer belong to us, no longer take part in our lives, no longer spring from the active, voluntary and personal side of our strength, but from the primitive, formless and enslaved being that affords us an entertainment as amusing as are all those in which we detect the play of the instinctive powers of nature. A movement of hatred, of selfishness, of silly vanity, of envy or disloyalty, when examined in the light of perfect sincerity, becomes nothing more than an interesting and singular flower. This sincerity, like fire, purifies all that it embraces. It sterilizes the dangerous leaven and turns the greatest injustice into an object of curiosity as harmless as a deadly poison in the glass case of a museum. Imagine Shylock capable of knowing and confessing his greed: he would cease to be greedy, and his greed would change its shape and no longer be odious and hurtful.

. . .

For the rest, it is not indispensable that we should correct our acknowledged faults; for there are faults that are, so to speak, necessary to our existence and our character. Many of our defects are the very roots of our good qualities. But the knowledge and admission of these faults and defects chemically precipitates their venom, which becomes no more than a salt, lying inactive at the bottom of the heart, whose innocent crystals we can study at leisure.

III

The purifying force of the avowal depends upon the quality of the soul that makes it and of the soul that receives it. Once that the balance is established, avowals raise the level of happiness and love. So soon as they are confessed, old lies or new, the most serious weaknesses change into unexpected ornaments and, like beautiful statues in a park, become the smiling witnesses and placid demonstrations of the clearness of the day.

We all desire to attain that blissful sincerity; but we are long fearful lest those who love us should love us less if we revealed to them that which we scarcely dare reveal to ourselves. It seems to us as though certain avowals would disfigure for ever the image which they have formed of us. If it were true that the avowals would disfigure it, that would be a proof that we are not loved on the same scale as that on which we love. If he who receives the avowal cannot rise to the height of loving us the more for that avowal, there is a misunderstanding in our love. It is not he who makes the avowal that should blush, but he who does not yet understand that we have overcome a wrong by the very act of confessing it. It is not we but a stranger who now stands in the place where we committed a fault. The fault itself we have eliminated from our being. It no longer sullies any save him who hesitates to admit that it sullies us no longer. It has nothing more in common with our real life. We are no longer anything but the accidental witness of it and no more responsible for it than a good soil is responsible for an ill weed or a mirror for an ugly reflection that passes across it.

IV

Let us not fear any the more that this absolute sincerity, this double transparent life of two beings who love each other, will destroy the background of shadow and mystery that must exist at the bottom of any lasting affection, nor that it will dry up the great unknown lake which, at the summit of every love, feeds the desire for mutual knowledge, the desire which itself is merely the most passionate form of the desire for greater love. No, that background is only a sort of movable and provisional scenery that serves to give to provisional loves the illusion of infinite space. Remove it, and behind it there will at last appear the genuine horizon, with the real sky and sea. As for the great unknown lake, we soon perceive that, until this day, we had drawn from it only a few drops of troubled water. It does not open on to love its healing springs until the moment of sincerity; for the truth in two beings is incomparably richer, deeper and less exhaustible than their appearance, reticence and lies.

V

Lastly, let us not fear that we shall exhaust our sincerity nor imagine that it will not be possible for us to attain its furthest limits. When we believe and wish it absolute, it is never more than relative; for it can manifest itself only within the borders of our conscience, and those borders are shifted every day, so that the act or thought which we present under the colours which we see in it at the moment of avowal may have an import quite different from that which we attribute to it to-day. In the same way, the act, thought or feeling which we do not avow, because we do not yet perceive it, may become to-morrow the object of a more urgent and graver avowal than all those which we have made to this hour.

PORTRAIT OF A LADY

A FRAGMENT - TRANSLATED BY ALEXANDER TEIXEIRA DE MATTOS.

... He said that the intelligence of this fair lady was like a diamond in a handsome setting.

— LA BRUYÈRE.

I

"She is beautiful," he said, "with that beauty which the years most slowly change. They transform it without diminishing it and in order to replace too fragile graces by charms that appear a little more grave and a little less touching only because we feel them to be more lasting. Her body promises to retain for long, until the first shock of old age, the pure and supple lines that dignify desire; and, without knowing why, we are sure that it will keep its promise. Her flesh, intelligent as a glance, is incessantly renewed by the mind that quickens it and dares not assume a wrinkle, displace a flower nor disturb a curve admired by love.

II

"It was not enough that she should be the one virile friend, the equal comrade, the nearest and deepest companion of the life which she had linked to her own. The star which would have her perfect and which she had learnt not to resist would also have her remain the lover of whom one wearies not. Friendship without love, like love without friendship, is but a half-happiness that makes men sad. They enjoy the one only to regret the other; and, finding but a mutilated joy on life's two fairest hill-tops, they persuade themselves that the human soul can never be perfectly happy."

III

"Around her summit, reason, the purest that can illumine a being, keeps watch; but it displays only the grace and not the effort of light. Nothing appeared to me colder than reason, until I had seen it thus play around the brow of a young woman like the lamp of the sanctuary in the hands of a laughing, innocent child. The lamp leaves nothing in the shade; but the harshness of its rays does not pass the inner circle of life, whereas their smiles beautify all that they touch without.

"Her conscience is so natural and so sound that we do not hear it breathe and that she appears unaware of its existence. She is inflexible towards the activity which she directs, but with such ease that she seems to be stopping to rest or to bend over a flower when she is with all her strength resisting an unjust feeling or thought. A movement, an ingenuous and sprightly phrase, a tear that laughs, dissembles the secret of the deep struggle. All that she has acquired has the grace of instinct; and all that is instinctive has become innocent. Of all the feminine passions, none has perished, none is a prisoner, for all are needed, the humblest and most futile and the greatest and most dangerous alike, to form the perfume that love loves to breathe. But, although not held in bondage, they live in a sort of enchanted garden, whence they do not dream of escaping, where they lose the desire to do harm and where the smaller and more useless, unable to remain inactive, amuse and divert the greater."

IV

"She has, therefore, by way of an adornment, all the passions and all the weaknesses of womankind; and, thanks to the gods, she does not present that still-born perfection which possesses all the virtues without being vivified by a single fault. In what imaginary world do we find a virtue that is not grafted upon a defect? A virtue is but a vice that raises instead of lowering itself; and a good quality is but a defect that has turned itself to use.

"How should she have the necessary energy if she were deprived of ambition and pride? How could she thrust aside unjust obstacles if she did not possess a reserve of selfishness proportionate to the lawful exigencies of her life? How should she be ardent and fond if she were not sensual? How should she be kind if she were not a little weak? How should she be trustful if she were not often too credulous? How should she be beautiful if she knew not mirrors and did not seek to please? How should she preserve her feminine grace if she had no innocent vanities? How should she be generous if she were not a little improvident? How should she be just if she were unable to be hard, how brave if she were not rash? How should she be devoted and capable of sacrifice if she never escaped from the control of icy reason? What we call virtues and vices are the same forces passing along a life. They change their name, according to the direction in which they go: to the left, they fall into the shallows of ugliness, selfishness and folly; to the right, they climb to the high lands of nobleness, generosity and intelligence. They are good or bad according to what they do and not according to the title which they bear."

V

"When a man's virtues are depicted for us, they are represented in the effort of action; but those which are admired in a woman always infer a model as motionless as a beautiful statue in a marble gallery. She is an inconsistent image, a tissue of vices quiescent, of inert qualities, of slumbering epithets, of passive movements, of negative forces. She is chaste because she has no senses, she is kind because she does harm to none, she is just because she does not act, she is patient and resigned because she is devoid of energy, she is indulgent because none offends her or forgiving because she has not the courage to resist, she is charitable because she allows herself to be stripped or because her charity deprives her of nothing, she is faithful, she is loyal, she is submissive, she is devoted because all these virtues can live in emptiness and can blossom on a dead woman's body. But what shall happen if the image takes life and comes forth from her retreat to enter upon an existence in which all that does not take part in the movement that surrounds it becomes a pitiful or dangerous wreck? Is it still a virtue to keep faithful to an ill-chosen or morally extinguished love, or to remain subject to an unintelligent or unjust master? Is to refrain from harming enough to make one kind, to refrain from lying enough to make one true? There is the morality of those who keep to the banks of the great river and the morality of those who ascend the stream. There is the morality of sleep and that of action, the morality of shadow and that of light; and the virtues of the first, which may be described as concave virtues, must needs arise, stand up and become virtues in relief, if they are to remain virtues in the second. The matter and the lines perhaps remain identical, but the values are exactly reversed. Patience, mildness, submissiveness, confidence, renunciation, resignation, devotion, sacrifice, all fruits of passive goodness, become, if we remove them, such as they are, into the stern outer life, no more than weakness, servility, indifference, unconsciousness, indolence, unconstraint, folly or cowardice and must, in order to keep at the necessary level the source of goodness from which they spring, be able to develop into energy, firmness, obstinacy, prudence, indignation and revolt. Loyalty, which has scarce anything to fear so long as it does not stir, must be careful lest it be duped and surrender its arms to the enemy. Chastity, which sat waiting with eyes closed and hands folded, has the right to change into passion, which shall decide and settle destiny. And the same consecutively with all the virtues which have a name as with those which are as yet unnamed. Next, it is a problem to know which is preferable, active or passive life, that which mingles with men and events or that which shuns them. Is there a moral law that imposes the one or the other, or has each the right to make his choice according to his tastes, his character, his aptitudes? Is it better or worse that the active or the passive virtues should stand in the foreground? It may, I think, be declared that the former always imply the second, but that the converse is not true. Thus, the woman of whom I speak is the more capable of devotion and sacrifice in that she has the strength to ward off their overwhelming necessity longer than any others. She will not cultivate sadness or suffering vaguely, as a means of expiation or purification; but she is able to accept and go in search of them with ingenuous ardour in order to save those whom she loves a small affliction or a great sorrow which she feels herself strong enough to face alone and to overcome in silence in her secret heart. How often have I not seen her force back tears ready to gush forth under unjust reproaches, while her lips, on which flickered a fevered smile, held back, with almost invisible courage, the word which would have justified her, but which would have crushed him who misjudged her. For, like all just and good beings, she had naturally to undergo the petty injustice and the petty wickedness of those who hover indeterminately between good and evil and who hasten to abuse the indulgence or forgiveness too frequently obtained. There you have that which, better than any slack and weeping acquiescence, shows an ardent and potent reserve of love."

VI

"Iphigenia, Antigone or sister of charity, like every woman, if need be, she will not ask Fate to wound her to the death, as though in order to be able at last, in the final struggle, to weigh the perhaps wonderful powers of an unexplored heart. She has learnt to know their number and their weight in the peace and certainty of her conscience. Apart from one of those tests in which life brings us to a standstill at the relentless barriers of a fatality or an inexorable natural law, she will instinctively take another road to reach the end pointed out by duty. In any case, her devotion and sacrifice will never be resigned, will never abandon themselves to the perfidious sweetness of sorrow. Ever upon the watch, upon the defensive, and full of strenuous confidence, she will to the last moment seek the weak spot in the event that is crushing her. Her tears will be as pure, as gentle as the tears of those who do not resist the insults of chance; but, instead of dimming her gaze, they will summon to it and multiply in it the light that consoles or saves.

VII

"For the rest," he added, in conclusion, "the Arténice whom I have endeavoured to depict to you will, under the features which I have given her, appear either perfectly hateful or perfectly beautiful according to the ideal which each of you carries within himself or believes himself to have met. There is no agreeing except on passive virtues. These have, from the point of view of painting, an advantage which the others do not enjoy. It is easy to evoke resignation, abnegation, submissiveness, virginal modesty, humility, piety, renunciation, devotion, the spirit of sacrifice, simplicity, ingenuousness, candour, the whole silent and often desolate group of woman's powers scared away into life's dim corners. The eye recognizes with emotion the familiar colours faded by the centuries; and the picture is always full of a plaintive grace. It would seem as if those virtues could not be mistaken, and their very excesses make them more touching. But what an unusual and ungrateful face is worn by those which stand out, which assert themselves and which struggle without the gates! A mere nothing, a stray lock, a fold of a garment that is not in its customary place, a tense muscle, makes them unpleasing or suspicious, pretentious or hard. Woman has so long lived kneeling in the shadow that our prejudiced eyes find it difficult to seize the harmony of the first movements which she risks when rising to her feet in the light of day. But all that one can say when striving to paint the intimate portrait of a being bears but a very imperfect resemblance to the more precise image which our thoughts form in our minds at the moment when we are speaking of him; and this last image, in its turn, is but a sketch of the great likeness, living, profound, but incommunicable, which his presence has imprinted in our heart, like the light on the sensitized plate. Compare the last proof with the first two: however exact, however well impressed we may think these to be, they no longer offer more than the garlands and arabesques of frames more or less appropriate to the subject which they await; but the genuine face, the authentic and integral being, with the only real good and evil which he contains beneath his apparently real vices and virtues, emerges from the shadow only at the immediate contact of two lives. The finest energies and the worst weaknesses add hardly anything to the mysterious entity that asserts itself, take hardly anything from it; and what is revealed is the very quality of its destiny. We then become aware that the existence which we have before us, all the hidden possibilities of which only pass through our eyes to reach our soul, is really that which it would wish to become, or will never be that which it loyally strives not to remain."

VIII

"If it matters much to friendship and love, it matters but little to our instinctive sympathy that some one should be good or bad, do good or ill, provided that we accept the secret force that animates him. That secret force often reveals itself at the first meeting; sometimes also we learn to know it only after long habit. It has scarce anything in common with the outward acts or even with the thoughts of the real person, who does not seem to be its exact representative, but its chance interpreter, by means of whom it manifests itself as best it may. Thus we have all of us, among those whom the see-saw of our days mingles with our existence, friends or associates whom we scarcely esteem, who have done us more than one ill office and in whom we know that we can have no confidence. Nevertheless, we do not bring ourselves to despise them as they deserve and to thrust them from our path. Across and in spite of all that separates us and all that disfigures them, an averment in which we place a more solid and more organic belief than in all the experience and all the arguments of reason, an obscure but invincible averment testifies to us that that man, were he to precipitate us into the most real and most grave misfortunes, is not our enemy in the general and eternal plan of life. It may be that there is no sanction for these sympathies and antipathies, and that nothing answers to them either among the visible or invisible phenomena of which our existence is made up, or among the known or unknown fluids that form and maintain our physical or moral health, our feelings of joy or sadness and the mobile and most impressionable medium in which our destiny floats. The fact none the less remains that there is here an undeniable force which plays a decisive part in the accomplishment of our happiness, both in friendship and in love. This third power has regard to neither age nor sex, neither beauty nor ugliness; it is independent of physical or sexual attraction and of affinities of mind and character. It is, as it were, the beneficent and generous atmosphere in which that attraction and those affinities bathe. To the absence of this third power, this vivifying atmosphere, from love are due all the misunderstandings, all the griefs, all the deceptions that disunite two beings who esteem, understand and passionately love each other. Since the nature of this power is unknown, it is given various obscure names. It is called the soul, the instinct, the unconscious or the subconscious, the divine even. It probably emanates from the undefined organ that binds us to all that does not directly concern our individuality, to all that extends beyond it in time and space, in the past and in the future."

THE LEAF OF OLIVE

TRANSLATED BY ALEXANDER TEIXEIRA DE
MATTOS.

I

*L*et us not forget that we live in pregnant and decisive times. It is probable that our descendants will envy us the dawn through which, without knowing it, we are passing, just as we envy those who took part in the age of Pericles, in the most glorious days of Roman greatness and in certain hours of the Italian Renascence. The splendid dust that clouds the great movements of men shines brightly in the memory, but blinds those who raise it and breathe it, hiding from them the direction of their road and, above all, the thought, the necessity or the instinct that leads them.

It concerns us to take account of this. The web of daily life varies little throughout the centuries in which men have attained a certain facility of existence. This web, in which the surface occupied by boons and evils remains much the same, shows through it either light or dark according to the predominant idea of the generation that unfolds it. And, whatever its form or its disguise may be, this idea always reduces itself, in the ultimate issue, to a certain conception of the universe. Private or public calamity and prosperity have but a fleeting influence on the happiness and unhappiness of mankind, so long as they do not modify the general ideas with which it is nurtured and enlightened on the subject of its gods, of infinity, of the great unknown and of the world's economy. Hence, we must seek there, rather than in wars and civil troubles, if we would know whether a generation have passed in darkness or in light, in distress or in joyfulness. There we see why one people, which underwent many reverses, has left us numberless evidences of beauty and of gladness, whereas another, which was naturally rich or often victorious, has bequeathed to us only the monuments of a dull and awe-struck life.

II

We are emerging (to speak only of the last three or four centuries of our present civilization), we are emerging from the great religious period. During this period, despite the hopes laid beyond the tomb, human life stood out against a somewhat gloomy and threatening background. This background allowed the thousand mobile and diversely shaded curtains of art and metaphysics to intervene pretty freely between the last men and its faded folds. Its existence was to some extent forgotten. It no longer appeared in view save at the hour of the great rifts. Nevertheless, it always existed in the immanent state, giving a uniform colour to the atmosphere and the landscape and giving to human life a diffuse meaning which proposed a sort of provisional patience upon questions that were too pressing.

To-day, this background is disappearing in tatters. What is there in its place to give a visible form, a new meaning to the horizon?

The fallacious axis upon which humanity believed itself to

revolve has suddenly snapped in two; and the huge platform which carries mankind, after swaying for some time in our alarmed imaginations, has quietly settled itself again to turning on the real pivot that had always supported it. Nothing is changed except one of those unexplained phrases with which we cover the things which we do not understand. Hitherto, the pivot of the world seemed to us to be made up of spiritual forces; to-day, we are convinced that it is composed of purely material energies. We flatter ourselves that a great revolution has been accomplished in the kingdom of truth. As a matter of fact, there has been, in the republic of our ignorance, but a permutation of epithets, a sort of verbal *coup d'État*, the words "mind" and "matter" being no more than the interchangeable attributes of the same unknown.

III

But if it be true that, in themselves, these epithets should have merely a literary value, since both are probably inaccurate and no more represent reality than the epithet "Atlantic" or "Pacific" represents the ocean to which it is applied, they do, nevertheless, according as we adhere exclusively to the first or to the second, exercise a prodigious influence over our future, over our morality and, consequently, over our happiness. We wander round the truth, with no other guide than hypotheses which light, by way of torches, some famous, but magic phrases, and soon those phrases become for us so many living entities, which place themselves at the head of our physical, intellectual and moral activity. If we believe that mind directs the universe, all our researches and all our hopes are concentrated upon our own mind, or rather upon its verbal and imaginative faculties and we become addicted to theology and metaphysics. If we are persuaded that the last word of the riddle lies in matter, we apply ourselves exclusively to interrogating this and we place our confidence in experimental science only. We are beginning, however, to recognize that "materialism" and "spiritualism" are merely the two opposite, but identical names of our impotent labour after comprehension. Nevertheless, each of the two methods drags us into a moral world that seems to belong to a different planet.

IV

Let us pass over the accessory consequences. The great advantage of the spiritualistic interpretation is that it gives to our life a morality, an aim and a meaning that are imaginary, but very much superior to those which our cultivated instincts proffer to it. The more or less unbelieving spiritualism of to-day still draws light from the reflection of that advantage and preserves a deep, though somewhat shapeless faith in the final supremacy and the indeterminate triumph of the mind.

The other interpretation, on the contrary, offers us no morality, no ideal superior to our instinct, no aim situate outside ourselves and no horizon other than space. Or else, if we could derive a morality from the only synthetic theory that has sprung from the innumerable experimental and fragmentary statements which form the imposing but dumb mass of the conquests of science, I mean the theory of evolution, it would be the horrible and monstrous morality of nature, that is to say, the adaptation of the species to the environment, the triumph of the strongest and all the crimes necessary to the struggle of life. Now this morality, which does, in the meanwhile, appear to be another certainty, the essential morality of all earthly life, since it inspires the actions of agile and ephemeral man as well as the slow movements of the undying crystals: this morality would soon become fatal to mankind if it were practised to an extreme. All religions, all philosophies, the counsels of gods and wise men have had no other object than to introduce into this overheated environment, which, if it were pure, would probably dissolve our species, elements that should reduce its virulence. These were, more particularly, a belief in just and dread gods, a hope of reward and a fear of eternal punishment. There were also neutral matters and antidotes, for which, with a somewhat curious foresight, nature had reserved a place in our own hearts: I mean goodness, pity, a sense of justice.

Wherefore, this intolerant and exclusive environment, which was to be our natural and normal environment, was never and probably never will be pure. Be this as it may, the state in which it is to-day offers a strange and noteworthy spectacle. It is fretting, bubbling and being precipitated like a fluid into which chance has let fall a few drops of some unknown reagent. The compensating principles which religion had added to it are gradually evaporating and being eliminated at the top, while at the bottom they are coagulating into a thick and inactive mass. But, in proportion as these disappear, the purely human antidotes, although oxydized through and through by the elimination of the religious elements, gain greater vigour and seem to exert themselves to maintain the standard of the mixture in which the human species is being cultivated by an obscure destiny. Pending the arrival of as yet mysterious auxiliaries, they occupy the place abandoned by the evaporating forces.

V

Is it not surprising, at the outset, that, in spite of the decrease of religious feeling and the influence which this decrease must needs have upon human reason, which no longer sees any supernatural interest in doing good, while the natural interest in doing good is fairly disputable: is it not surprising that the sum of justice and goodness and the quality of the general conscience, far from diminishing, have incontestably, increased? I say incontestably, although doubt-less the fact will be contested. To establish it, we should have to review all history, or, at the very least, that of the last few centuries, compare the position of those who were unhappy formerly with that of those who are unhappy now, place beside the sum total of the injustice of yesterday the sum total of the injustice of to-day, contrast the state of the serf, the semi-serf, the peasant, the labourer, under the old systems of government, with the condition of our working-man, set the indifference, the unconsciousness, the easy and harsh certainty of those who possessed the land in former days against the sympathy, the self-reproachful restlessness, the scruples of those who possess the land to-day. All this would demand a detailed and very long study; but I think that any fair mind will, without difficulty, allow that there is, notwithstanding the existence of too much real and widespread wretchedness, a little more justice, solidarity, sympathy and hope, not only in the wishes of men—for thus much seems certain—but in very deed....

To what religion, to what thoughts, to what new elements are we to attribute this illogical improvement in our moral atmosphere? It is difficult to state precisely; for, though it is certain that they are beginning to act in a very perceptible manner, they are still too recent, too shapeless, too unsettled for us to qualify them.

VI

Let us, nevertheless, try to pick out a few clues; and let us state, in the first place, that our conception of the universe has been greatly and most effectively modified and, above all, that it is tending to become modified more and more rapidly. Without our accounting for it, each of the numerous discoveries of science—whether affecting history, anthropology, geography, geology, medicine, physics, chemistry, astronomy or the rest—changes our accustomed atmosphere and adds some essential thing to an image which we do not yet distinguish, but which we see looming above us, occupying the whole horizon, and which we feel, by a presentiment, to be enormous. Its features are straggling, like those illuminations which we see at evening fêtes. A frontal, colonnade, cupola and portico, all incoherent, appear abruptly in the sky. We do not know what they mean, to what they belong. They hang absurdly in the motionless ether; they are inconsistent dreams in the still firmament. But, suddenly, a little line of light meanders across the blue, and, in the twinkling of an eye, connects the cupola with the columns, the portico with the frontal, the steps with the ground; and the unexpected edifice, as though flinging aside a mask of darkness, stands affirmed and explicit in the night.

It is this little line of light, this deciding undulation, this flash of general and complementary fire that is still lacking in the night of our intelligence. But we feel that it exists, that it is there, outlined in shadow in the darkness, and that a mere nothing, a spark issuing from we know not what science will be enough to light it and to give an infallible and exact sense to our immense presentiments and to all the scattered notions that seem to stray through unfathomable space.

VII

Meanwhile, this space—the abode of our ignorance—which, after the disappearance of the religious ideas, had appeared frightfully empty, is gradually becoming peopled with vague, but enormous figures. Each time that one of these new forms uprises, the boundless extent in which it comes to move increases in proportions that are boundless in their turn; for the limits of boundlessness evolve in our imagination without ceasing. Assuredly, the gods who conceived certain positive religions were sometimes very great. The

Jewish and Christian God, for instance, declared Himself incommensurable, containing all things, and His first attributes were eternity and infinity. But the infinite is an abstract and tenebrous notion which assumes life and is explained only by the displacing of frontiers which we thrust back further and further into the finite. It constitutes a formless extent of which we can acquire a consciousness only with the aid of a few phenomena that start up on points more or less distant from the centre of our imagination. It is efficacious only through the multiplicity of the, so to speak, tangible and positive faces of the unknown which it reveals to us in its depths. It does not become comprehensible and perceptible to us until it shows animation and movement and kindles on the several horizons of space questions more and more distant, more and more foreign to all our uncertainties. For our life to take part in its life, the infinite must question us incessantly and incessantly place us in the presence of the infinity of our ignorance, which is the only visible garment beneath which it allows us to conjecture the infinity of its existence.

Now the most incommensurable gods hardly put questions similar to those which are endlessly put to us by that which their adorers call the void, which is, in reality, nature. They were content to reign in a dead space, without events and without images, consequently without points of reference for our imagination, and having only an immutable and immobile influence over our thoughts and feelings. Thus, our sense of the finite, which is the source of all higher activity, became atrophied within us. Our intelligence, in order to live on the confines of itself, where it accomplishes its loftiest mission, our thought, in order to fill the whole space of our brain, needs to be continually excited by fresh recallings of the unknown. So soon as it ceases to be daily summoned to the extremity of its own strength by some new fact—and there are hardly any new facts in the reign of the gods—it falls asleep, contracts, gives way and sinks into decay. One thing alone is capable of dilating equally, in all their parts, all the lobes of our head, and that is the active idea which we conceive of the riddle in the midst of which we have our being. Is there danger of error in declaring that never was the activity of this idea comparable with that of to-day? Never before, neither at the time when the Hindoo, Jewish or Christian theology flourished, nor in the days when Greek or German metaphysics were engaging all the forces of human genius, was our conception of the universe enlivened, enriched and broadened by proofs so unexpected, so laden with mystery, so energetic, so real. Until now, it was fed on indirect nourishment, so to speak, or rather it fed illusively on itself. It inflated itself with its own breath, sprinkled itself with its own waters, and very little came to it from without. To-day, the universe itself is beginning to penetrate into the conception which we form of it. The diet of our thought is changed. That which it takes comes from outside itself and adds to its substance. It borrows instead of lending. It no longer sheds around itself the reflection of its own greatness, but absorbs the greatness around it. Until now, we had been prosing, with the aid of our infirm logic or our idle imagination, on the subject of the riddle; to-day, issuing from our too inward abode, we are trying to enter into relations with the riddle itself. It questions us, and we stammer as best we may. We put questions to it, and, in reply, it unmasks, at moments, a luminous and boundless perspective in the immense circle of darkness amid which we move. We were, it might be said, like blind men who should imagine the outer world from inside a shut room. Now, we are those same blind men whom an ever-silent guide leads by turns into the forest, across the plain, on the mountain and beside the sea. Their eyes have not yet opened; but their shaking and eager hands are able to feel the trees, to rumple the spikes of corn, to gather a flower or a fruit, to marvel at the ridge of a rock or to mingle with the cool waves, while their ears learn to distinguish, without needing to understand, the thousand real songs of the sun and the shade, the wind and the rain, the leaves and the waters.

VIII

If our happiness, as we said above, depends upon our conception of the universe, this is, in a great measure, because our morality depends upon it. And our morality depends much less upon the nature than upon the size of that conception. We should be better, nobler, more moral in the midst of a universe proved to be without morality, but conceived on an infinite scale, than in a universe which attained the perfection of the human ideal, but which appeared to us circumscribed and devoid of mystery. It is, before all, important to make as vast as possible the place in which are developed all our thoughts and all our feelings; and this place is none other than that in which we picture the universe. We are unable to move except within the idea which we create for ourselves of the world in which we move. Everything starts from that, everything flows from it; and all our acts, most often unknown to ourselves, are modified by the height and the breadth of that immense well of force which exists at the summit of our conscience.

IX

I think that we may say that never was that well larger nor more highly placed. Certainly, the idea which we shape for ourselves of the organization and government of the infinite powers is less precise than heretofore; but this is for the good and noble reason that it no longer admits of falsely-defined conventional limits. It no longer contains any fixed morality, any consolation, any promise, any certain hope. It is bare and almost empty, because nothing subsists in it that is not the very bedrock of some primitive facts. It no longer has a voice, it no longer has images, except to proclaim and illustrate its immensity. Outside that, it no longer tells us anything; but this immensity, having remained its sole imperious and irrefutable attribute, surpasses in energy, nobility and eloquence all the attributes, all the virtues and perfections with which we had hitherto peopled our unknown. It lays no duty upon us, but it maintains us in a state of greatness that will permit us more easily and more generously to perform all those duties which await us on the threshold of a coming future. By bringing us nearer to our true place in the system of the worlds, it adds to our spiritual and general life all that it takes away from our material and individual importance. The more it makes us recognize our littleness, the greater grows that within us which recognizes this littleness. A new being, more disinterested and probably closer to that which is one day to proclaim itself the last truth, is gradually taking the place of the original being which is being dissolved in the conception that overwhelms it.

X

To this new being, itself and all the men around it now represent only so inconsiderable a speck in the infinity of the eternal forces that they are no longer able to fix its attention and its interests. Our brothers, our immediate descendants, our visible neighbour, all that but lately marked the limit of our sympathies, are gradually yielding precedence to a more inordinate and loftier being. We are almost nothing; but the species to which we belong occupies a place that can be recognized in the boundless ocean of life. Though we no longer count, the humanity of which we form a part is acquiring the importance of which we are being stripped. This feeling, which is only beginning to make its way in the accustomed atmosphere of our thoughts and of our unconsciousness, is already fashioning our morality and is doubtless preparing revolutions as great as those wrought in it by the most subversive religions. It will gradually displace the centre of most of our virtues and vices. It will substitute for an illusory and individual ideal a disinterested, unlimited and yet tangible ideal, of which it is not yet possible to foresee the consequences and the laws. But, whatever these may be, we can state even now that they will be even more general and more decisive than any of those which preceded them in the superior and, so to speak, astral history of mankind. In any case, it can hardly be denied that the object of this ideal is more lasting and, above all, more certain than the best of those which lightened our darkness before it, since it coalesces on more than one point with the object of the universe itself.

XI

And we are just at the moment when a thousand new reasons for having confidence in the destinies of our kind are being born around us. For hundreds and hundreds of centuries we have occupied this earth; and the greatest dangers seem past. They were so threatening that we have escaped them only by a chance that cannot occur more than once in a thousand times in the history of the worlds. The earth, still too young, was poising its continents, its islands and its seas before fixing them. The central fire, the first master of the planet, was at every moment bursting from its granite prison; and the globe, hesitating in space, wandered among greedy and hostile stars ignorant of their laws. Our undetermined faculties floated blindly in our bodies, like the nebulæ in the ether; a mere nothing could have destroyed our human future at the groping hours when our brain was forming itself, when the network of our nerves was branching out. To-day, the instability of the seas and the uprisings of the central fire are infinitely less to be feared; in any case, it is unlikely that they will bring about any more universal catastrophes. As for the third peril, collision with a stray star, we may be permitted to believe that we shall be granted the few centuries of respite necessary for us to learn how to ward it off. When we see what we have done and what we are on the point of doing, it is not absurd to hope that one day we shall lay hold of that essential secret of the worlds which, for the time being and to soothe our ignorance (even as we soothe a child and lull it to sleep by repeating to it meaningless and monotonous words), we have called the law of gravitation. There is nothing mad in supposing that the secret of this sovereign force lies hidden within us, or around us, within reach of our hand. It is perhaps tractable and docile, even as light and electricity; it is perhaps wholly spiritual and depends upon a very simple cause which the displacing of an object may reveal to us. The discovery of an unexpected property of matter, analogous to that which has just disclosed to us the disconcerting qualities of radium, may lead us straight to the very sources of the energy and the life of the stars; and from that moment man's lot would be changed and the earth, definitively saved, would become eternal. It would, at our pleasure, draw closer to or further from the centres of heat and light, it would flee from worn-out suns and go in search of unsuspected fluids, forces and lives in the orbit of virgin and inexhaustible worlds.

XII

I grant that all this is full of questionable hopes and that it would be almost as reasonable to despair of the destinies of man. But, already, it is much that the choice remains possible and that, hitherto, nothing has been decided against us. Every hour that passes increases our chances of holding out and conquering. It may be said, I know, that, from the point of view of beauty, enjoyment and the harmonious understanding of life, some nations—the Greeks and the Romans of the commencement of the Empire, for instance —were superior to ourselves. The fact none the less remains that the sum total of civilization spread over our globe was never to be compared with that of to-day. An extraordinary civilization, such as that of Athens, Rome or Alexandria, formed but a luminous islet which was threatened on every side and which ended by being swallowed up by the savage ocean that surrounded it. Nowadays— apart from the Yellow Peril, which does not seem serious—it is no longer possible for a barbarian invasion to make us lose in a few days our essential conquests. The barbarians can no longer come from without: they would issue from our fields and our cities, from the shallow waters of our own life; they would be saturated with the civilization which they would lay claim to destroy; and it is only by making use of its conquests that they would succeed in depriving us of its fruits. There would, therefore, at the worst, be but a halt, followed by a redistribution of riches.

Since we have a choice of two interpretations, forming a background of light or of shade for our existence, it would be unwise to hesitate. Even in the most trivial circumstances ... of life, our ignorance very often offers us only a choice of the same kind, and one which does not impose itself more strongly. Optimism thus understood is in no way devout or childish; it does not rejoice stupidly like a peasant leaving the inn; but it strikes a balance between what has taken and what can take place, between hopes and fears, and, if the last be not heavy enough, it throws in the weight of life.

For the rest, this choice is not even necessary: it is enough that we should feel conscious of the greatness of our expectation. For we are in the magnificent state in which Michael Angelo painted the prophets and the just men of the Old Testament, on that prodigious ceiling of the Sistine Chapel: we are living in expectation and perhaps in the last moments of expectation. Expectation, in fact, has degrees which begin with a sort of vague resignation and which do not yet hope for the thrill aroused by the nearest movements of the expected object. It seems as though we heard those movements: the sound of superhuman footsteps, an enormous door opening, a breath caressing us, or light coming; we do not know; but expectation at this pitch is an ardent and marvellous state of life, the fairest period of happiness, its youth, its childhood....

I repeat, we never had so many good reasons for hope. Let us cherish them. Our predecessors were sustained by slighter reasons when they did the great things that have remained for us the best evidence of the destinies of mankind. They had confidence when they found none but unreasonable reasons for having it. To-day, when some of those reasons really spring from reason, it would be wrong to show less courage than did those who derived theirs from the very circumstances whence we derive only our discouragements.

We no longer believe that this world is as the apple of the eye of one God who is alive to our slightest thoughts; but we know that it is subjected to forces quite as powerful, quite as alive to laws and duties which it behoves us to penetrate. That is why our attitude in the face of the mystery of these forces has changed. It is no longer one of fear, but one of boldness. It no longer demands that the slave shall kneel before the master or the creator, but permits a gaze as between equals, for we bear within ourselves the equal of the deepest and greatest mysteries.